Jim Eldridge

LONDON STORIES

■ SCHOLASTIC

While the events described and some of the characters in this book may
be based on actual historical events and real people, the Baker children are
fictional characters, created by the author, and their stories are works of fiction.

Scholastic Children's Books
Euston House, 24 Eversholt Street,
London, NW1 1DB, UK
A division of Scholastic Ltd

London ~ New York ~ Toronto ~ Sydney ~ Auckland
Mexico City ~ New Delhi ~ Hong Kong

First published in the UK by Scholastic Ltd, 2012

Text copyright © Jim Eldridge, 2012

ISBN 978 1407 12195 6

CONTENTS

Fire and sword! AD 61   7

Assassin! 1066   21

Death at the Globe Theatre 1587   41

The Gunpowder Plot 1605   69

The Great Fire 1666   89

Escape from the Tower of London 1716   107

The slave trade 1790   137

Young Charles Dickens 1824   153

Royal duty 1868   177

Blitz! 1940   193

World Cup final 1966   213

Olympic dreams 2012   231

London Stories

This is the story of a city: my city, London. It is where I was born; in my case in Camden Town, a mile to the north of Euston station in the heart of London. I lived in Bayham Street, the street Charles Dickens once lived in. It's the place I grew up, whose streets and boroughs I explored at length: by bus if travelling far, but usually on foot (we Londoners walked nearly everywhere in those days). Since then I have lived in many other places, but I will always be a Londoner; it is in my genes, in my bones; it is a city that echoes through every part of me.

The tales of this city are told through the eyes of children, because that is how I saw it. These are imagined stories, but based on real people, real events that happened in one of the oldest and most historical cities in the world. Some think the city dates back to Roman times, but it dates back much, much farther than that.

So, where to begin? Maybe with the river, the Thames, England's longest river, meandering and twisting for 215 miles from its source in the hills of Gloucestershire, before it heads out through the wide estuary into the cold waters of the North Sea.

It was here on an area of marshy ground on the banks of the Thames, just before the river widened and became the estuary to the sea, that Stone Age people settled hundreds of thousands of years ago. Here, they hunted wild animals, many of them long since extinct in Britain: mammoth, elephants, hippopotami, reindeer, bears, buffalo, hyenas, rhinoceros, beavers.

Time passed. During Neolithic times land was cleared and levelled for farming. Wooden trackways were built across the marshes and swamps linking thatched houses. Communities sprang up.

More time passed: the Bronze Age came and went, followed by the Iron Age. By 400 BC most people in Britain were speaking a kind of Celtic or Gaelic.

At the same time the Roman Empire was expanding, and more Celts came to Britain as refugees, fleeing the Romans. Most settled in the south-east in the place that had already become a thriving settlement: a trading place, a port, a town on a river – London.

Where did the name come from? Some say the Romans were the first to name it, calling it Londinium; but I'm sure they're wrong. There was a town here long before the Romans came, and it had a Celtic name, Lunndon (which roughly translates as *the town on the marshy place*).

In 55 BC the Roman Emperor, Julius Caesar, decided that he wasn't content with the Roman Empire ending at the sea in northern Gaul (now France); he'd set his sights on the island of Britannia. So the Romans invaded and Britannia, including Lunndon, was claimed as part of the Roman Empire. That done, the Roman forces departed, leaving the Celts to their own devices.

It was not until almost a hundred years later, in AD 43, that the

Emperor Claudius sent another army to invade Britannia. This time the Romans stayed, and it was at this time that *Lunndon* became *Londinium*.

By AD 61, Londinium was a Romano-British city, with mixed-race soldiers who had retired from the Roman army marrying local British women and settling down as New Britons. At first it was an uneasy mix, as times of new immigration often are, with some suspicion and hostility between Romans and Celts, but the expanding city of Londinium was able to cope and became a melting pot of peoples and tribes and races.

But in the eastern region of Britannia (now East Anglia), where the Iceni tribe lived, hostilities between the garrisoned Romans and the native Britons reached a bloody climax. In AD 61 the king of the Iceni, Prasutagus, died, and the local Roman Governor of the province took everything that had belonged to the late king for himself, breaking a treaty between the Britons and the Romans. Furious, Prasutagas's widow, Queen Boudicca, led the Iceni in rebellion against the Romans. They attacked the capital of the area, Colchester, killing all the Romans and Romano-British, and destroyed the city. After Colchester, Boudicca turned her attention to the major centre of Roman trade, the Roman heart of Britain: Londinium.

Fire and sword! AD 61

Twelve-year-old Bran stood on the hill and looked towards the city in the distance: Londinium, where the hated Romans kept British women and children in wooden pens, like cattle, before selling them as slaves. Once sold, they were loaded onto ships in chains and transported abroad, sometimes as far as Rome. Bran knew this to be true because he'd heard it from others in the huge army that now gathered along the crest of the hill. The army of Boudicca, queen of the Iceni. An army that had already driven the Romans out of their city of Colchester and laid it to waste, killing everyone within its walls and destroying the whole city with fire.

After the destruction of Colchester, the massive army had moved on, heading south towards Londinium, driving the Romans ahead of them, terrified and running for their lives. All the time Boudicca's army grew ever larger as more Britons joined, bringing with them their own weapons: spears, swords, bows, slings. Some brought carts to help transport the supplies. They were of all kinds and all ages: strong warriors, old men and women, mothers with children, often whole families, all with one aim – to drive the Romans out of Britain.

The Romans had arrived in Bran's small village in the east of Britain just before he was born. Bran's father had died fighting the Roman invaders, as had many of the men in the village. The Romans fought protected by clothes made of metal, unlike the British warriors who fought naked. The Romans also had a bigger array of weapons. And there had been masses of them against just a handful of tribesmen. Bran's father's heroism had been to no avail. The Romans had won, and conquered Bran's village, just as they'd conquered other nearby towns and villages.

The Romans took the grain the villagers grew; they took the animals raised for food. It was true they hadn't taken *all* the grain and animals, just what they called a tax. But the things the Romans took had made life harder for the Britons.

When the Romans first arrived there had been attempts to drive them out, Bran was told, but the Britons had always been defeated. The Romans were stronger, more disciplined and better trained, with better weapons. And finally, the attempts at rebellion died out, and the Britons got on with life. The Romans were just another hardship to endure – until the king of Bran's tribe, Prasutagus of the Iceni, died. There was talk that he had been killed by the Romans. Whether that was true or not, what *was* true was that after Prasutagus died the Romans tried to take complete control of the area where the Iceni lived. Until then, the Romans had shared control with Prasutagus. At least, that was supposed to have been the situation. To Bran it seemed the Romans had always had absolute control.

Once Prasutagus was dead, the Roman Governor of the region had the King's widow, Boudicca, arrested. To show his power, and the might of Rome, he had her and her children beaten. They say he was going to have them killed and their heads put on poles. But Boudicca had always been a strong queen. She attacked and killed the Romans guarding her. Then she called her own guards together and they launched an attack on the Romans.

Word spread about what was happening, and some Iceni warriors rushed to help her. Soon the whole area of the Iceni had risen up in revolt. Bran had joined Boudicca's army, determined to avenge the death of his father and pay the Romans back for the years of hardship. Bran's mother, Oona, had wished him well, but had chosen to stay at their home in the village.

Now, after weeks of fighting and killing and looting, Boudicca's army had the Roman stronghold of Londinium itself in their sights. Soon they would attack.

Eleven-year-old Shona stood in her father's bakery and appealed to him desperately.

"We have to leave, Father!"

Her father, Dumno, concentrated on pounding the mass of dough with his fists.

"Do you hear me, Father?" begged Shona. "The rebel army is gathering outside the city! They'll kill us! People are fleeing. Whole families!"

"They won't kill *us*," retorted Dumno. "We're Britons. They're seeking revenge on Romans."

"They're killing everyone who stands in their way."

"But we *don't* stand in their way," insisted Dumno. "I'm just a baker. I'm no warrior!"

"You bake bread for the Romans," insisted Shona.

"Yes, because they pay me," snapped back Dumno. "I also bake bread for any Britons who want it, although most seem to want to make their own," added Dumno sourly. "There's no living to be made baking bread for Britons."

"The rebels will see us as traitors," implored Shona. "Boudicca says that any Briton who trades with the Romans is a traitor."

Dumno scowled and spat on the ground.

"Yet she and her husband traded with the Romans long enough!" he said. "All of them, the Iceni, the Trinovantes, they were happy to take the Romans' money."

Dumno was from the Atrebates tribe. For as long as he could remember, and even far back in his grandparents' times, the different tribes of Britain had been at war with one another. Until the Romans arrived – then suddenly they all had a common enemy. But despite this enemy, many of the tribes still kept their deep-rooted mistrust of one another.

"Father, we *must* leave *now*!" begged Shona. "The Romans will have fled. There will be no one to sell bread to!"

"I'll sell it to Boudicca and her army," said Dumno. "An army has

10

to eat, and they won't have had time to bake bread on the march. Now go and bring in another sack of flour. I should be working instead of engaging in this foolish chatter!"

Shona hesitated, wondering if she should press her father some more, tell him how important it was that they left, but she could tell from the set of his shoulders as he kneaded the dough that he wouldn't listen to her. Her father was stubborn and fixed in his ways. He baked bread, and nothing or no one would stop him from doing it. Even when Shona's mother had died the year before, Dumno had taken just half a day away from his bakery – he'd buried his wife, and returned to his oven.

Shona went outside to the flour store. Many of the houses around them were empty; their neighbours had fled southwards or westwards to escape the oncoming rebel army. *We are Britons, we will be safe*, said her father, but Shona was not so sure.

The Romans who lived in Londinium did not seem so bad to Shona. Most of them were merchants, and merchants thought of only two things: business and money. They did not care who or where it came from; Briton or Roman or Gaul, it was all the same. Yes, it was true some sold Britons as slaves, but then so did some of the British chiefs. Shona and her parents had made a good living from her father's bakery, mainly because of the Romans. But now that living was over. Their lives would be over, unless they left the city.

"We can always return later," Shona had said to her father only the previous day, "once the rebel army has gone."

"Return to what?" her father had asked stubbornly. "To a house and bakery destroyed by that rabble? No!"

Shona felt helpless. She wished her mother were still alive. *She* would have been able to persuade her husband to leave. But since her mother had died, Dumno had become bitter and even more stubborn.

Shona looked towards the north. Even from this great distance, she could see the shapes of Boudicca's army. Thousands and thousands of them, massed together. She couldn't make out the carts or the people, but she could see their banners flying above them on poles, and saw the sunlight glint on the blades of their swords and their spears. The rebels waited there, on the hills overlooking Londinium, like a flock of black crows.

"We are going to die," Shona muttered to herself fearfully. "We are all going to die."

There was a feeling of readiness among Boudicca's rebels. The camp was packed away, the animal skins that gave them cover from the night cold had been folded and piled onto the carts; the blades of the weapons had been sharpened; the horses had been fed and watered. In the early morning light, envoys from Boudicca's Iceni tribe were moving amongst the crowd, reminding them of the glorious victory at Colchester, and how, all the way to Londinium, the Romans had run in terror before them.

"The Romans are dogs and cowards!" raged the envoys. "They butcher women and children. They've taken the food from our mouths for too long. This day we'll drive them out of Britain for ever!"

And then Bran saw Boudicca herself, in her chariot, her two daughters by her side, making her way through the ranks of the rebels to take her position at the front of her army. Her long yellow hair was tied back with a leather thong and hung right down to her hips, over her long cloak. The dawn sunlight glistened on the large golden torc she wore around her neck. Beside her, her daughters were dressed in warrior costumes of leather. Sticking up from the sides of the chariot were three poles, each with a head on – Roman heads, now decaying, the flesh falling away where the carrion birds had torn at them.

Boudicca's chief warriors ran alongside her chariot, waving their spears and swords and shouting. They were virtually naked, their bodies adorned with patterns painted in blue woad, mystic symbols to give them protection against the enemy.

Bran's heart swelled with pride at the sight of the Iceni queen and her chief warriors. He was one of her soldiers! While Boudicca led them, they couldn't fail. He pulled out his long knife, which he'd sharpened proudly, in readiness.

Boudicca's chariot was now at the very front of her army. Before her there was only Londinium. She drew back on the reins, pulling her horses to a halt. Then she raised her sword high.

"Britannia!" she shouted, her strong voice echoing over the crowd.

"Britannia!" they shouted back, taking up her cry.

And then she flicked the reins and roared. Her chariot surged forward, down the hill, and the rest of her army poured after her.

13

"They're coming!"

Shona ran into the bakery, twisting her hands together in fear.

Dumno sighed.

"Then we won't sell any bread today," he said.

"It's not about selling bread!" Shona shouted desperately at him. "It's about staying alive! We have to run!"

Once more, Dumno shook his head.

"We'll go out and welcome them," he said. "They'll see we're Britons. We'll be safe." He took a large cloth and laid it over the dough he had prepared. "There," he said. "Now we're ready."

Boudicca's forces swept through the houses at the edge of the city, slicing everything before them with their swords, and thrusting their spears. All the while the sound continued: a mix between a bird's warble and a shrieking scream, coming from the massed hordes who filled the carts and ran behind the warriors at the front.

"Kill them all!" shouted Boudicca, and it spread through her army like a deadly chant.

In the press of the crowd that followed behind the front-line warriors, Bran felt his throat tighten and his chest swell. The Romans were running! They were afraid! But then he saw that not all the people were Romans – many had the pale skin and red hair of Britons. When Boudicca's army had taken Colchester, and when it had destroyed the legion that fought them by the River Stour, those had all been Romans.

"They're Britons!" said Bran to the man nearest him, horrified.

"They're Romans!" snarled the man, brandishing his spear. "They're Britons who wanted to be Romans, anyway. Let them die with their Roman friends!"

This is blood lust, thought Bran. Anger had been replaced by a taste for killing and power.

As the horde swept into the city Bran saw a man step out from a small house. The man was dusty with flour. It was on his face and in his hair, on the smock he wore.

"Britons—" began the man.

The rebel next to Bran rushed at the flour-dusted man and thrust his spear at him with all his force. The spear went right through the flour-dusted man. He stumbled back, his eyes wide, and as he fell to the ground, he tried to call out: "Sho…"

The angry Briton pulled his spear out. The dusty man screamed again as the blade ripped backwards through his body, and then he slumped down in a pool of blood.

Bran ran to the fallen man and knelt beside him. He was dead. Around him, the mob surged onwards, shouting and screaming, flailing and attacking everything in their path. Bran could see more people being killed ahead of him, some turning to run but being hacked down. Some were Roman, but many more were Britons.

We are killing our own kind, thought Bran with horror.

He looked towards the house from where the dead man had come. Were there others inside there? Holding his knife at the ready, alert for an attack, Bran approached the house carefully. The door was open. He stepped inside.

It was a bakery. The table was covered with a dusting of flour. The oven was aglow. The room itself was empty. No, it *seemed* empty but Bran was sure there was someone here, hiding. It was a sixth sense, an instinct he'd developed from being with Boudicca's army, the awareness of being on guard at all times – listening out for the slightest noise in case it might be an enemy creeping up on him.

He stood in the empty room, listening. Outside the war cries and shrieks were still going on, both from Boudicca's fighting warriors and their victims. He tried to cut out the outside sounds and focused on the room he was in. There was someone here, he could feel it. Was it a fighter? Someone lying in wait for Boudicca's army to enter?

Then he heard a slight noise. It came from behind a curtain. Bran moved softly towards the curtain, his knife ready to plunge forwards. He reached the curtain, took hold, and then jerked it suddenly back, and found himself looking down into the terrified face of a girl of about his age.

"Don't kill me!" she begged.

Bran pulled the curtain back wider. The girl's clothes were also covered in flour, and there was flour specking her red hair.

"I won't," he said gently.

"We aren't Romans," said the girl. "My father and I are Britons."

Her father. The flour-dusted man lying dead outside.

"Your father is dead," he said.

There was no other way to tell her. He could pretend, and find soft words, but then she would go outside and see the body lying in its own blood. She needed to be prepared.

She nodded, and then began to cry.

"I warned him," she said between sobs. "I told him we had to flee. But he said that we were safe because we were Britons."

"No one is safe," said Bran. He reached down and took her hand, and helped her to her feet. "My name is Bran," he said. He looked around the room. "Your father was a baker?"

The girl nodded, doing her best to stop her tears.

"I … I helped him, with the bread," she said.

Outside, the sounds of the rebel army were becoming distant as they moved on, ever deeper into the city.

"When this is over," said Bran, "the city will need bread."

"That's what my father said," agreed Shona. She hesitated, then she said, "My name is Shona."

Shona, thought Bran. That's what the man had been trying to say, to warn her.

"I heard him call out, just before he died," Bran told her. "Your name was the last word he said."

Shona was still crying, but quietly now, her smock pressed against her face to muffle her tears. Finally she put down her smock and looked around the room, her tear-streaked face suddenly blazing with defiance.

"I'll bake the bread," she said. "My father's work will go on!"

"You'll need help," said Bran.

"I'll find help!" said Shona, the look on her face more determined than ever.

"If you teach me, I'll help you," offered Bran.

Even as he said it, he surprised himself. *I am a warrior*, he thought. Then he realized: *No. I was happy to be a warrior against the Romans. But I don't kill Britons.*

Shona looked at him, studying him, thoughtfully. Then she nodded and said: "We'll be bakers."

"Yes," nodded Bran. "We'll be bakers."

And so Bran and Shona became bakers. And, as time passed, they became more than just workers making bread – they became a couple, and then a family. The family from which sprang all the Bakers in these pages: one family growing and spreading.

Meanwhile, the rebellion led by Boudicca continued. After her army had destroyed London, they continued northwards on what is now the A5, set on driving the Romans out of Britain. On their way north, Boudicca's army laid waste to the Romano-British town of Verulanium (St Albans), before meeting the Roman Governor, Paulinus, and his army at Mancetter, which Paulinus had chosen for his stand against Boudicca. Paulinus had just 10,000 Roman soldiers against Boudicca's 250,000, but by pitting strict Roman military discipline against Boudicca's angry but less disciplined force, the Romans won the battle.

To make sure that there were no further uprisings, Paulinus carried out a ruthless "fire and sword" policy of destruction against the British tribes afterwards, and the Roman military presence was increased. As a result, the Romans ruled Britain for the next 400 years, until the Roman Empire began to crumble.

The Romans left Britain in about AD 450. The next 500 years were turbulent times for Britain, and for London, with wave after wave of invaders.

First came the Angles, Saxons, Franks and Jutes from continental Europe. In the 6th century, the Angles and Saxon invaders created a new settlement called Lundunwic, about a mile to the west of the site of the old Roman city of Londinium. Lundunwic was in that area of London north of the Thames from the Strand, covering what is now Covent Garden. When the Vikings arrived in the 9th century they took over this city and renamed it Ealdwic (now called Aldwych in central London).

By the 10th century most of the warring tribes of Britain had united into one nation under a series of Anglo-Saxon kings, culminating in Edward the Confessor, who came to the throne in 1043. It was Edward the Confessor who ordered the building of Westminster Abbey in stone.

The new Westminster Abbey was consecrated on 28 December 1065, just one week before Edward the Confessor died and was succeeded by Harold II. But William of Normandy claimed Harold had promised the crown of England to him, and launched an invasion.

The Saxon King, Harold, found himself fighting on two fronts: against King Harold Hardrada of Norway in the north (who was supported by Harold's brother, Tostig); and against William of Normandy in the south. After defeating Harold Hardrada and Tostig at Stamford Bridge in Yorkshire, Harold brought his army south to face the invading army of William of Normandy at a site near Hastings. Harold was killed and William the Norman was victorious.

Assassin! 1066

"I'll kill him! I'll kill the Norman!"

"Hush now, Edmund!" Alfred the Baker stopped kneading the dough and turned to his young son, who pummelled the dough on the bench as if he was punching an enemy. "These are dangerous times! Don't say those words out loud."

"Why not?" demanded Edmund angrily. "That man isn't our king! The Normans don't rule us!"

"They do," said his father sadly. "Ever since King Edgar surrendered…"

"He was a coward!" raged Edmund.

"He was your king!" snapped Alfred in reprimand. "I will not hear you say such things against him!"

"If he was our king, why is he still alive?" countered Edgar. "He didn't even fight against the Normans! He wasn't there when King Harold died. When…" His voice broke, and Alfred could hear the tears in his son's voice, ready to burst out. "When Wilfred died."

Wilfred, Alfred's oldest son, who'd fought alongside King Harold at Hastings, and been killed in the battle.

Alfred sighed and put his arm comfortingly around his son's shoulders.

"That's life, Edmund," he said gently. "Kings fight, and many of those who fight with them die. Your brother was a brave warrior. He died defending our country. But now he is dead. King Harold is dead. Edgar the Atheling has sworn loyalty to the Norman King, as have the bishops and the barons, and all those who *did* fight. They see that the war is lost."

"The war is never lost!" burst out Edmund. "We shall throw these Norman invaders out!" He turned to his father, a look of desperate appeal on his face. "If King Harold hadn't had to fight the Vikings and those traitors in the north…"

"Yes, he would have been able to face William with a fresh and strong army, rather than one tired after marching four hundred miles in just a few days, and with the marks of battle still upon them," nodded his father. Then his tone hardened as he added: "But he *did* face William with a tired army. And he lost. It may not be fair, it may not be right, but that's the way life is. Sometimes we win. Sometimes we lose. This time we lost, and now we have a new king…"

"*I* don't have a Norman for a king!" shouted Edmund. "And I won't make bread for his coronation! Not unless I can poison it!"

With that, the angry boy ran from the bakery and out into the street. Alfred was on the point of shouting after him, calling him back, but what was the point? Edmund was angry. No, more than that, Edmund was consumed by hatred. His beloved elder brother was dead, and Alfred knew he'd never forgive the Normans for that. It was pointless to argue that Wilfred had volunteered, that he'd *chosen* to fight.

"Edmund is troubled?"

Alfred turned and saw that Edith, his eleven-year old daughter and the youngest of his children, was standing in the doorway that led to their living quarters.

Alfred sighed and shook his head.

"He's more than troubled," he said gloomily. "He's filled with the desire for revenge against the Normans." He looked at the heaps of dough on the bench in front of him. "He thinks I'm betraying Wilfred because I'm baking bread for the coronation celebrations. But what am I to do? It's my job! And I'm not just baking it for the Normans to eat. Our own barons and bishops will be at the celebrations." He gave a long miserable sigh. "That's just the way life is. We have to go on."

Edmund sat on the stone step and looked across at Westminster Abbey. Why did they live here? What had made his great-grandfather set up his bakery business here of all places, right by the Abbey? The place where the tyrant, the murderer, the invader, the Norman, would be crowned king of England in just a few days. If his family bakery had been anywhere else in London he could walk away from it, pretend the coronation wasn't happening. It made him sick. He wanted to spit into the bread so that those Normans chewed on his phlegm. If he was lucky he'd be spitting disease into the bread, and they'd die. But then, if that happened, they would know it was the bread that had killed them, and his father would be arrested and executed.

So what? His father was a traitor! By baking bread for the enemy, his father was betraying his own people, and most of all, the memory of his own dead son!

"You look sick, Edmund," said a voice.

Edmund looked up. Two boys stood there, Eric and Oswald. They were older than him, but had been considered too young to fight in King Harold's army.

"I am sick," replied Edmund. "Sick of making bread for the invader!"

"If we'd been there," Eric said, "at Hastings, us and others like us, the tyrant wouldn't have won. We'd have shown the Norman how true Saxon warriors would stand against him!"

"The Saxons did stand against him!" burst out Edmund angrily. "My brother was there and he died, and bravely!" He groaned and his head sank down. "But there weren't enough men!"

The two older boys looked down at the bowed unhappy figure of Edmund and exchanged awkward looks. Then Oswald said quietly: "There is a plan."

Edmund scowled.

"A plan?" he echoed sarcastically. "What plan? A plan to hold dances in the new k ing's honour?"

There was a silence, then Oswald whispered: "To kill the Norman." As soon as he'd spoken the words, he looked around, to make sure that he hadn't been overheard.

Edmund looked at the two boys, searching their faces to see if they were making a joke, or spinning a tale. But he could tell by the anxious expressions on their faces that this was no joke or fanciful story. He got to his feet.

"Whose plan?" he demanded. "How? When?" And then, feeling his heart almost bursting with a desire for revenge, "What can I do?"

Edith crouched behind the wall and listened. She had followed Edmund when he'd left the bakery, worried that he might do something foolish. Instead he'd met up with those friends of his, and what was happening now was even worse than she'd imagined. The two boys were outlining a plan to kill King William.

"An archer is going to do it," said the taller of the two, Oswald. "He's an excellent marksmen and can knock the eye out of a hare at fifty paces."

"He fought alongside King Harold at Stamford Bridge, but was wounded there and didn't travel back to Hastings," added Eric.

"The problem is that on the day the Norman is to be crowned, no person carrying a bow or weapon of any sort will be allowed anywhere near to the Abbey except the Norman soldiers. So his bow and arrows need to be hidden in place, ready for the day," said Oswald. "And because the Normans are going to be suspicious of any adults carrying anything that might look like a weapon for a few days before the coronation, the plan is for boys like us to bring the bow here and hide it, ready for him."

"Boys *like* us?" queried Edmund.

There was a pause, and the three boys exchanged awkward looks. Then Eric said quietly: "Us. We're doing it."

"The bow will be wrapped in cloth, as will the arrows, so that no one will know what they are," said Oswald.

"We're to pick them up tomorrow and take them to the hiding place."

"Count me in," said Edmund grimly.

Crouched behind the wall, Edith was filled with horror. She wanted to leap up and shout out, "No!" Instead, she stayed where she was. She heard the two older boys make arrangements to meet Edmund later, and when she'd heard them leave and was sure they were out of earshot, she stood up.

"You idiot, Edmund!" she burst out.

Edmund jumped.

"Edith!" he stammered. "What … what were you doing?"

"Listening!" she told him, angrily. "The same as any Norman could have done!" She shook her head, tears in her eyes. "Edmund, don't be a fool!"

The shock had gone from Edmund's face, and now his expression hardened.

"We have to get rid of this invader," he said. "And this is the only way." He stepped towards his sister, the look on his face threatening. "But don't tell Dad," he said warningly. "If he knows, then he'll be as much at risk as everyone else."

With that, Edmund walked off. Edith watched him go, her heart in her mouth. What could she do? If she told her father, then Alfred would have the terrible choice of having his own son arrested and killed or saying nothing and letting the murder go ahead. And if that happened, she knew the Normans would wreak a terrible revenge on the whole of London.

That night, as she lay in bed, Edith couldn't sleep. Every time she closed her eyes she had visions of the assassin's arrow thudding into King William, and Edmund being arrested and tortured, and finally hanged, drawn and quartered for treason.

I can't let it happen! she thought. *I have to stop it! But how?*

She could tell her father, but she didn't know who the assassin was, or where he'd be firing his arrows from.

The next morning when she joined her father for breakfast he looked at her, concerned.

"You look ill, Edith," he said. "I heard you restless during the night, moving about and groaning. Do you have pains?"

Edith shook her head. She knew that her father was afraid the sweating sickness that had taken her mother might kill her, too.

"No, Father," she said. "It was just a stomach upset. Nothing more."

Her father still looked worried.

"Your mother's illness began with a stomach upset," he said. He looked pointedly at the piece of bread on her platter that lay untouched. "She couldn't eat."

"I'm fine," insisted Edith. She picked up the piece of bread and began to chew at it, even though the nervousness inside her made her want to be sick.

"Where is Edmund?" she asked. "Is he still asleep?"

Her father shook his head.

"He left early," he said, sighing heavily. "He slipped out before it was even light."

"Where?" asked Edith sharply, a feeling of panic rising in her.

Alfred shrugged.

"I didn't ask," he said. "To be honest, little one, it's easier for me when he's out of this place. At least I don't have to put up with him scowling at me all the time."

Desperately, Edith forced down the rest of the bread.

"I have to go out, Father," she said.

"Where?" asked her father, concern once again in his voice. "The streets are dangerous at this time, Edith, with William's coronation tomorrow. The Normans are worried that some might use the opportunity to rise up against William, so their soldiers are patrolling the area, rounding up likely troublemakers."

"I'll be all right, I promise," said Edith. "It's just that I told Mother Magred that I'd call on her and see if she needed any herbs gathered."

"The Wise Woman," nodded Alfred. "Well, while you're with her perhaps you'd ask her to look at you and make sure you're not ill."

"I will, Father," said Edith.

Once she had left the bakery, Edith hurried towards the Abbey.

As her father had said, the streets were filled with Norman soldiers, pushing their way through the crowds and checking the stalls that had been set up to sell goods during the crowning of the new King. Edith reached the Abbey and stood scanning the crowds for any sign of Edmund, or Eric and Oswald. They were nowhere to be seen.

Think! Edith urged herself. *The assassin won't be able to get into the Abbey, so he'll be outside. Because of the crowds, he'll have to be somewhere where he can fire his arrow over their heads. Somewhere high.*

She looked up at the windows of the long row of buildings opposite the entrance to the Abbey. She was sure it would be one of those, somewhere where he'd have a clear shot. But which one?

The Normans had set up a guard outside the Abbey, a line of soldiers making sure that only authorized people went in and out. They weren't risking an assassin getting into the Abbey ahead of the coronation. Edith guessed that the inside of the Abbey was already well-protected by more soldiers.

Other soldiers appeared from the side streets where the market stalls were being set out. They were armed with swords and spears, ready to strike if needed.

They know that there are many who hate them, thought Edith. *Despite the Saxon Barons and nobles swearing allegiance, they are on their guard. William is no fool; he wouldn't have become so powerful and all-conquering if he was.*

Then she saw Edmund. He was pushing his way through the crowds on the opposite side of the street to the Abbey, Eric and Oswald walking

29

with him. They were carrying bundles of long twigs and branches each, tied up, and strung with ivy and holly. They looked as if they were carrying decorations for the coronation, but Edith knew they weren't. She watched as the three boys walked past the Norman soldiers on guard outside the Abbey, and then headed for the door of one of the houses opposite. So that's the house where the assassin will be hiding, Edith thought. She looked up at the window on the top floor. It offered a perfect view of the entrance to the Abbey.

From what she'd heard as the boys plotted, they would bring the assassin's bows and arrows to the house and leave them there in readiness for him. Either very early tomorrow, or possibly later that night, the assassin would arrive.

I have to act *now*, thought Edith. As soon as Edmund and the others have gone, I'll get into the room and cut the string of the bow and break the arrows. There'll be no time for the assassin to get more.

Edith hung about in the busy street, her eyes on the door to the house, but keeping to the shadows of the buildings and the bustling crowds so that Edmund wouldn't see her when he came out.

The three boys weren't in the house for long. Eric was first out, followed by Oswald, and then Edmund. They were empty-handed. They'd delivered the assassin's weapons, and now they hurried away.

Edith waited until they were well out of sight, gone down the side roads where the stalls were set out; then she hurried to the house. She pushed open the door and stepped inside, and stood there, listening. She could hear voices coming from the room nearby, a woman and children chattering. But Edith's destination was the room upstairs that looked out onto the main street.

She mounted the stairs carefully, hearing them creak beneath her feet. She reached the landing. The door to her right was the one that led to the first floor room with a view onto the main street. She put her ear to the door and listened. There was no sound from within. She knocked at the door. She had already made up her story if anyone answered her knock she was looking for Mother Magred, the Wise Woman. But no one called to her from inside the room; there was no sound.

Edith pushed open the door and looked in. There were just a few sticks of furniture in the room, a sack mattress on the floor but there was no sign of the bundles of twigs that disguised the bow and arrows.

Not this room, then. That meant it had to be the room on the next floor up, at the top of the house.

Edith pulled the door shut and climbed the stairs to the top floor. She went to the door of the room overlooking the street and, as before, put her ear to the door and listened and then knocked at the door. As before, there was no answer.

Edith pushed open the door, and saw the bows and arrows leaning up against the window. She hurried inside and began to strip the ivy from the twigs so she could get at the arrows and the bow beneath. She wished she had a knife with her to make the job easier, and considered going back to her father's bakery and fetching one. But she knew there was no time to lose. If she was going to save Edmund from being caught up in a plot that could lead to his execution, she needed to act *now*.

"What are you doing?"

The gruff voice nearly made her faint with shock. Edith turned, and saw a tall man standing in the doorway. He was dressed in a leather jerkin and had a dreadful scar down one side of his face.

"I … I …" stammered Edith.

The man came into the room and shut the door, his eyes fixed grimly on her.

"I'm making sure everything's all right," she said.

The man shook his head.

"No you're not," he said. "You're a spy!"

"No!" protested Edith. "I … I … I was the one who brought these here."

The man stared at her, shocked. Then he laughed.

"A girl your size carrying these?" he chuckled. "I don't think so!" He untied a length of rope from round his waist. "And the fact you know so much about what's here worries me."

"I don't know!" protested Edith. "I just came here looking for Mother Magred, the Wise Woman."

"And instead you found these, and me," said the man.

Suddenly his hand shot out. Edith tried to dodge, but he was too fast. His gnarled fingers dug into her arm, and she cried out in pain.

"An archer's fingers," said the man, "are tough as leather. You can bite them and claw at them, but you'll never break his grip."

"I didn't mean anything, please don't hurt me!" begged Edith.

"I won't hurt you," said the man.

Before Edith could move or struggle, he had wrapped the rope around her wrists and tied them tightly together. Then he pushed her down to the bare floorboards and tied her ankles together with another length of rope.

"There," he said. "Now, you can tell me who you are and what you are doing here?"

"I … I'm Edith Baker," said Edith. "I live not far away."

"And why did you come here?"

"I wanted to get a good view of the coronation tomorrow," said Edith. "I'm only small and I wouldn't be able to see through the crowds in the street."

The man studied her thoughtfully, then nodded.

"That's a good story," he said. "Believable." Then he shook his head. "It's a pity you didn't tell me that one first – I might even have believed you. But earlier, you told me you brought these" – he gestured at the bow and arrows concealed among the twigs and foliage – "which makes me wonder how you knew about them."

"I heard someone talking about them," said Edith. "I was curious."

"Someone talking about them?" asked the man, looking at her intently. "Who?"

"I don't know," said Edith. "Some boys."

"And they talked about bringing them here?"

Immediately Edith became worried. If she said any more, then it was likely that Edmund would be in dreadful trouble with this man.

"No," she said. "I followed them."

"Then you are a spy!" accused the man.

"No!" said Edith. "I was just … curious."

The man studied Edith for a while, his eyes searching her face. Finally, he said: "I don't know whether you are telling the truth or not. Whatever the matter, I know I can't trust you to be let loose, knowing what you do."

"I won't say anything!" insisted Edith.

"Not before I finish my job, you won't," said the man. "You'll stay here the night, with me. And, when I've gone, someone will surely find you. Until then, to make sure you don't call out…"

"I won't–" began Edith, but her words were cut short as the man took a dirty rag from his pocket and tied it round her mouth, gagging her.

"No," said the man, standing up, "you won't."

Edith sat on the floor, her back against the wall, bound and gagged, and watched the man as he unwrapped the twigs and foliage and revealed a longbow and arrows. What could she do? Nothing, she admitted to herself with a sinking heart.

Her father would be wondering where she was. But then, he'd be very busy with baking bread for the next day's coronation.

She thought about Edmund. Would he wonder where she had disappeared to, especially once night fell and she didn't return home?

She watched as the man tested the bow, then looked down into the street below. He would be checking the entrance to the Abbey knowing that the Norman king would be arriving at that exact spot tomorrow. Edith wondered if the Norman would have his soldiers keep close around him to shield him. But then she remembered what she had been told about the famous Battle at Hastings: how there had been a rumour that William had been killed. To prove it was a lie, William had taken off his helmet and carried on into battle bareheaded, so that everyone could see his face and recognize him. Such a man would not hide behind his soldiers on the day of his coronation as the new king of England. He would make sure that everyone saw him. He would stand apart from his soldiers, dressed in all his finery. He would be an easy target for a good archer. She remembered Oswald's words: "He's an excellent marksmen and can knock the eye out of a hare at fifty paces."

Night fell. The archer sat down on the floor at the opposite side of the room and looked at Edith. He took a hunk of bread and cheese from his pocket.

"You can eat if you promise you will not call out," said the man. "Do you promise?"

Edith nodded. The man got to his feet. "If you try calling out, I shall break your neck with my hands," he told her. "We archers have got very strong hands."

He undid the gag from around Edith's head, and she eagerly sucked in air. The man untied her wrists and handed her a piece of the bread and cheese.

Although she was hungry, Edith ate slowly, not just to savour every mouthful, but to spin out the time before her wrists were tied together again, and the gag was fixed over her mouth.

"Don't think I'll fall asleep," the man told her. "I've spent too many nights in battle wide awake, waiting for the enemy."

Edith didn't give any sign of response, just sat, bound and gagged once more, and looked towards the window. The room was dark now, but moonlight filtered through, as well as an orange glow from the street. She assumed that the soldiers had lit braziers by the Abbey to help keep them warm while they kept watch overnight. Tomorrow would be a big day for the Normans: a Norman would be crowned king of England. Unless the man with the scarred face carried out his plan.

Edith was determined to remain awake through the night, just in case the archer fell asleep at any point. If that happened, she planned to drag herself out through the door of the room, and then bump down the stairs. But the archer was as good as his word. He didn't sleep. In the end it was Edith who slept. She woke to the sounds of people shouting outside in the street. She looked up and saw the man standing by the window, holding his bow, and placing an arrow in it. He looked at her.

"You're awake at last," he said. "You're just in time to see the invader die." He looked again out of the window, at the Abbey entrance. "Not that you'll actually see him die, not from there. But you'll know it's happened." He turned his attention to her and said solemnly, "I never miss."

There was a sudden roar from the street, and the sound of horses' hooves. The man turned his attention to the window.

"He's coming," he whispered. "The advance guard has just arrived." He shook his head. "These Normans love to make a show of themselves. With all his finery, he'll make a fine target."

The man raised his bow, the arrow notched.

No! thought Edith. This mustn't happen! The man pulled the bow string back slowly and strongly with his thick fingers.

Suddenly, Edith pushed herself to her feet and threw herself towards the man, rolling hard as she hit the floor. She felt herself hit the man in the legs. She heard the "twang" of the bowstring as the arrow was released, and then a shout from outside in the street. Had the arrow struck home? Was the Norman king dead?

But the shouting continued, and Edith realized they weren't shouts of horror but acclaim. The new king was being welcomed.

The archer pushed Edith aside and snatched up another arrow, notched it, and swung his bow up to the open window, pulling back on the string. As he did so, Edith once again rolled herself swiftly over the floor and cannoned into his ankles.

This time the archer turned on her, his face contorted into a snarl, the arrow in his bow aimed at her.

"No!"

Edith turned towards the shout of desperation. Edmund stood in the doorway, anguish on his face. The archer hesitated, then pulled his bow string back, the arrow still pointed directly at Edith … but there was a blur as Edmund hurled himself across the room and crashed into the man. There was a twang, and the arrow embedded itself in the wooden floorboards close by Edith's head.

The next second Edmund was climbing on the man, pulling at his hair, and punching him.

"Help!" yelled Edmund. "Help!"

The man stumbled back, and then his fist lashed out and smashed into the side of Edmund's head. As Edmund fell to the floor, the man dropped his bow and ran for the door. They heard his footsteps rushing down the stairs. Outside in the street the joyous shouting and celebrations continued, and the bells of the Abbey began to ring.

Edmund sat up, holding the side of his head in pain. He looked at Edith, then reached out and pulled the gag from her mouth.

"What are you doing here?" he demanded.

"I came to save you," she said. "What are you doing here?"

Edmund hesitated, then whispered, "I came to help kill the Norman."

"Why didn't you?" asked Edith.

Edmund crawled over to Edith and began to untie the ropes that bound her.

"Because I've already lost my brother to this war. I didn't want to lose my sister to it as well."

As the ropes relaxed, Edith rubbed her wrists and ankles.

"I'm sorry, Edmund," she said. "I know you hate me for messing this up, but it's because I love you."

Edmund shook his head. "I don't hate you," he sighed. "There'll be times when I do – but, for now, let's go and find Dad."

1066–1587

The coronation of William the Conqueror took place on Christmas Day, 25 December 1066. After the ritual crowning had taken place, the crowd outside the Abbey began to shout to show their approval, but unfortunately – due to language problems - the Norman soldiers on duty misinterpreted their shouts as anti-William and attacked the crowd, even going as far as setting fire to the nearby buildings to prevent a rebellion.

After the conquest of 1066, the Normans increased their grip on England, and in particular on London. The Tower of London was built to protect the Normans from possible rebellion by the Anglo-Saxons.

The next five hundred years saw battles for the crown of England between brothers and cousins. At times it was like a family squabble spilling over into a war as, for example, the sons of William the Conqueror, Robert and Henry, went to war with one another, both claiming they were the true King. Later, the cousins Matilda and Stephen, both claiming to be descendents of William, and therefore the rightful heir to the throne, went to war for eighteen years.

However, a form of peace finally came to the country when Henry VIII became king in 1509, and when his daughter Elizabeth became queen, England, and especially London, entered a new era of prosperity.

By the mid 16th century, London was at the heart of a major global Empire as England's leading sailors, including Sir Francis Drake and Sir Walter Raleigh, travelled the world and claimed the parts of the world they discovered for England in the name of Queen Elizabeth I.

At the same time, Spain was expanding her own Empire across the seas, and claiming them not just for Philip of Spain, but for the Catholic faith. Because after Elizabeth's father, Henry VIII, had broken away from the Catholic Pope to establish the Protestant Church of England, the Pope was desperate to bring England back into the Catholic fold.

To the Pope, the figure of the Protestant Elizabeth on the throne of England was a threat to the power of the Catholic Church. In 1570 the Pope issued an order authorizing the assassination of Elizabeth, and the placing of a Catholic on the throne of England in her place.

Death at the Globe Theatre 1587

"A pigeon's skull!" shouted Richard Burbage. "Which rancid varlet brought in this pigeon's skull?!"

There was a difficult sort of silence as we all stood around in the audience pit and looked up at the great actor as he stomped around the stage holding the skull of a pigeon.

"Come on!" he raged. "One of you dolts is responsible. Which one is it, or do I have to sack the whole lot of you?"

The awkward silence continued, and then I gritted my teeth and raised my hand.

"I did," I said, and all the others breathed a sigh of relief as they realized they'd been let off the hook. As Burbage glared at me and opened his mouth to let rip, I came in quickly with my defence.

"It wasn't my fault!" I protested. "In the script it just calls it a skull. It doesn't say anything about it being a *human* skull. It's the writer's fault. He should have made it clearer."

"What d'you mean, you arrogant little turkey-cock?" snapped a voice from behind me. It was the writer, William Shakespeare. I hadn't seen him standing just a few feet away.

"Hold it, Will," said Burbage from the stage. "I'm the leader of this company of players. I do the official telling off."

Turning back to me, Burbage lifted the pigeon's skull in his hand as if he was about to chuck it at me.

"In this play I'm to be fearful afraid because a skull appears before me and tells me my dreadful fortune. The audience should shudder with terror when they see the skull." He brandished the pigeon's skull. "They won't shudder when this puny thing appears. They'll laugh!"

With that he tossed the small skull into the air, then gave it a kick as it came down that sent it right up into the gallery, where the rich people sit to watch the play. It was a pretty good kick.

"Right," Burbage continued, now talking to everyone. "Back here at ten o'clock tomorrow morning for rehearsal."

Out of the corner of my eye I saw William Shakespeare bearing down on me, already rolling up his sleeve as if he was going to give me a belting for criticizing his writing. Luckily Burbage called out to him, "Will, I need you to talk about some re-writes. I need a few jokes in the Second Act when I come on first, otherwise the audience will get bored and start throwing turnips at me."

I made my hasty escape along with the others before Shakespeare could find an excuse to get away from Burbage. As I stepped out of the Globe Theatre into the street the sneery voice of Edgar Wilson said, "Fancy bringing in a pigeon's skull! I still think Burbage will sack you tomorrow."

"Burbage isn't going to sack anyone," I snapped back. "For one thing, none of us have been paid in weeks, so he can't afford to sack any of us in case we demand our back wages. The only one likely to get the order of the boot is you, because you're such a terrible actor."

Wilson glared at me and for a moment I thought he was actually going to start a fight. Then he just sniffed in that sneery way of his, and said, "I'm not going to fight you because I might damage my face. The audience expect to see me looking beautiful, not to have the sort of bashed-in face you've got."

With that he moved smartly away before I could kick him.

I set off along the road, doing my best to dodge the stream of urine (and worse) that rained down from the upstairs windows as people emptied their chamber pots into the street.

Grudgingly, I had to admit that there was some truth in what Wilson had said. All the women's and girls' parts in plays had to be played by either girlish-looking boys or young men. With my broken nose and my largish chin, if they'd put me on stage as a beautiful princess the audience would have died laughing. So instead I, Henry Baker, ten years old and with a face like a dog that had hit a wall at some speed, was doomed to play The Messenger or The Ugly Young Witch Who Doesn't Get Any Lines. I also acted as Assistant Stage Manager for Burbage's company of players, the Chamberlain's Men, which is why I'd got into trouble over that rotten pigeon's skull.

Where could I get my hands on a real human skull? I wondered if anyone who wouldn't be missed had died recently. No, that was no good – it needed to be an old skull. If I brought in a freshly-dead head I'd be in even more trouble with Burbage.

I was just passing a narrow alleyway, wondering how I was going to lay my hands on a skull that didn't have bits of flesh still on it, but one that also looked vaguely human, when I heard a voice from somewhere down the alley whisper: "The queen must die!"

I should have ignored it. All I had to do was just carry on walking and I would have probably forgotten all about it. But I'm inquisitive. Nosey, my mam calls it.

I stopped there at the end of the alley, straining my ears to listen and see if whoever it was said anything else. But there was nothing else. Whoever had spoken had either vanished into thin air, or had nipped through a door into a tavern or house.

I stood there, trying to work out where the whispering had come from. I was standing there, studying the doors when suddenly one of them opened and a big fat man wearing a leather apron came out. In his hand was a large bloodstained knife.

"What do you want?" he demanded.

I gulped, and then gave him a friendly smile.

"I'm looking for a head," I said.

A few minutes later I was heading back towards the Globe. Under my arm I carried a skull wrapped in a piece of bloodstained cloth. This one was a sheep's skull. All right, it wasn't a human skull, but it was bigger than a pigeon's. The butcher who opened the door had given it to me, and I didn't like to say "No thanks". I make a point never to argue with people, especially if they're holding weapons and look like they know how to use them.

As I walked through the door of the theatre, Robert Armin was on the stage on his own, trying out a piece of new comedy business with his dog. Every company had its own comedian, and Armin was ours. Armin stopped getting Fido to pretend to bite his ankle when I wandered in. He must have seen the nervous expression on my face because he asked, "Still worried Burbage will sack you over a paltry pigeon's skull, boy? It's unlikely."

"No," I said. And then, before I knew what I was doing, I blurted out what I'd just heard.

Suddenly the smile vanished from Armin's face.

"Nonsense!" he said. "You must have misheard!"

"I didn't!" I insisted. "So I went down the alley…"

"Don't tell me!" shouted Armin suddenly. "I refuse to be drawn into stories of supposed plots like this!" He called, "Come, Fido!", and walked out, Fido trotting at his heels.

I sighed. From listening to what my mam and dad said, ever since Elizabeth had become queen of England there had been plots and counter-plots, all aimed at getting rid of her and putting someone else on the throne of England. Every now and then another plot was uncovered and a few more people would die. The scheming lords and nobles would go to the Tower of London and have their heads chopped off, and the ordinary people caught up in it would just be stabbed to death. Then their heads would be stuck on spikes on the walls of the city as a warning to anyone else thinking of overthrowing the queen. Anyone even remotely connected with the traitors was suspected from that moment on. And being under suspicion was a very dangerous spot to be in.

I decided to slip out the back way. I headed towards the dressing room. I was just passing the door, when I felt rather than saw a movement behind me. A second later, a strong hand was placed over my mouth to stop me from yelling, and an arm caught me across the throat!

I bit hard, sinking my teeth into the hand covering my mouth. As my unseen assailant fell away from me, crying in pain, I leapt from him and turned around. It was William Shakespeare! He was hopping about, blowing on his hand.

"Master Shakespeare!" I gasped.

Immediately I felt a sense of relief. This wasn't an assassin, just a playwright upset because I'd criticized his stage directions about the skull.

"I'm sorry," I began. "I didn't realize it was you. And I promise never again to make any comments about the way you write your plays…"

"Shut up, you witless oaf!" snapped Shake speare, who had now recovered. "Tell me exactly what you heard!"

"Heard?" I gulped.

"Yes, as you were telling Armin, before that cowardly poltroon shut you up."

"W-well," I stammered. "That was all I heard. Someone whispered, 'The queen must die.'"

"Where was this?" demanded Shakespeare.

"In the alley that runs at the back of Cripplegate Lane."

Shakespeare fell silent and I could almost see his brain working for a moment. Then he said, "Come with me!"

"Where?" I asked suspiciously.

"There is someone I need you to talk to, urgently," he said.

"Oh no!" I said. "I'm as loyal to the queen as anybody, but I'm not getting involved! I don't know anything about any conspiracy!"

"Walk with me," ordered Shakespeare firmly.

And so we walked. After half an hour we arrived at an ordinary-looking house in Pudding Lane.

"In," ordered Shakespeare curtly.

We walked up some stairs and into a room where a posh-looking man sat at a desk, studying some papers.

"Who is this, and why is he here?" demanded the man.

"He is a boy actor in my company," replied Shakespeare. "His name is Henry Baker." Turning to me, he said: "Tell this gentleman what you heard."

Once again I told my story.

"It fits with the other information we have picked up lately," put in Shakespeare. "That there is a new plot to assassinate the queen. Now we have a voice. And a place for the conspirators."

"A voice that only this boy has heard," returned the bearded man.

"Exactly," said Shakespeare. "Somewhere in one of those houses in Cripplegate Lane is the owner of that voice. And Henry Baker can recognize it."

"Yes," nodded the man thoughtfully. Turning to me he said, "Boy, you will visit every tavern and lodging house in Cripplegate Lane until you hear that voice again."

"And what do I do if I find him?" I asked.

"You will tell Master Shakespeare." The man leant towards me threateningly. "And *only* Master Shakespeare. You will not tell anyone else about this affair. Nor about our meeting. Nor about this house. If you do, that will be counted as treason. Do you understand?"

I nodded.

Back outside in the bright light of day, I asked Shakespeare who the man was, and what was going on.

"That was Lord Walsingham, and you are now a member of Her Majesty's Secret Service," declared Shakespeare.

I spent that evening going in and out of the taverns along Cripplegate Lane. The Lobster's Head, The King's Arms, The Bucket, The Red Feathers, The Smelly Parrot, and many more that didn't even have names. It was on my second visit to The Bucket, as I was pushing my way through the crowds, pretending to look for my father, that I heard a voice mutter quietly, "The ale in this place tastes worse than vomit." I stiffened. It was exactly the same voice, using exactly the same tone. Speaking low.

I turned and saw the speaker. He was sitting in a corner seat, surrounded by a motley collection of men. Some were obvious thugs, with scarred faces and broken noses, there just to give the man protection. But he, and the man sitting next to him, were different. Both were bearded, and beneath their cloaks I could see that their clothes were rich and costly. The man who had spoken put his tankard down on the table with an expression of disgust. I studied him closer. A long nose, pinched at the sides. A long face. Black hair curling over his ears. His beard long, with touches of ginger and red among the black.

The man he was with had darker skin and a black beard, clipped much closer to his chin.

On an impulse I grabbed the arm of a woman who was going around the tavern collecting empty tankards.

"Those two men over there," I asked, nodding my head in their direction. "Who are they?"

The woman looked, then shrugged.

"How should I know?" she said. "They're just customers. Customers are money, not names. At least, that's what the boss says."

As she wandered off I thought that if that really was her boss's opinion, this place wouldn't be in business much longer. Especially if, as the man said, the ale here tasted so bad. Worse than vomit, he'd said.

Now I'd found the suspect, the sooner I handed the information to Shakespeare and got out of this business, the better. I was heading towards the door to get out of the tavern and do just that, when a heavy hand fell on my shoulder. I turned, and came face to face with two of the thugs who had been protecting the men in the corner. Instinctively I shot a glance at the corner, and saw that the two men had gone.

49

"Someone wants to have a word with you," said one of the thugs.

"What about?" I asked.

"He'll tell you that himself," replied the thug. "Come on." And he began to pull me towards a door at the back of the tavern.

"There must be some mistake," I protested. "I don't want to see anyone! I'm only here looking for my father!"

"Well you can carry on looking after you've had a word with t his gentleman," said the thug.

I was going to protest a bit more, and struggle, but it was a waste of time. The two thugs were a lot bigger and stronger than I was, and no one in the tavern seemed at all bothered to see a boy being dragged away by a couple of ugly ruffians.

I found myself being pushed through a door into a small back room. The owner of the mystery voice was sitting, waiting for me. Someone else stood behind him. Not his swarthy-faced companion with the black beard, but another man who had been sitting at the table with them. This man was younger and had no beard.

"Well well," said the bearded man. "I hear that you were asking my name?"

At the sight of my shocked look, he gave a cold smile. "I pay people to listen out for me. They heard you ask the woman. So, why do you want to know who I am?"

"Because…" I stammered, thinking quickly, "because I thought you were an actor," I gabbled.

The bearded man frowned, obviously puzzled.

"An actor?" he echoed.

"Yes," I nodded enthusiastically. "Your handsome looks, your rich voice. I was sure I had seen you on the stage." I threw in a smile, hoping it looked the sort of smile that theatre fans wore when greeting their favourite actor. "I am with a stage company myself. The Chamberlain's Men. Master Burbage's company. Maybe you have seen us...?"

"Quiet!"

The man had stopped looking puzzled and now just looked annoyed. He turned to the younger fellow standing beside him.

"Do you know this boy?" he asked.

The younger man shook his head.

"No," he said. "Maybe it's as he says. I hear that actors are very popular these days. Everyone wants to meet them."

"Perhaps," said the bearded one. "Though to mistake *me* for an actor is such an insult I've a good mind to kill him myself."

The other man laughed at this joke, and I joined in, hoping to let him know that I thought he was a very humorous chap. Our laughter was cut short when he rapped out: "Kill him and throw him in the river."

"Kill him?!" said the younger man, shocked.

"Kill me?!" I said, even more shocked. "But I'm an actor! They need me for our new play!"

"We can't kill him," protested the younger man. "He may be telling the truth."

"And he may not be. Didn't you hear him say he was with the Chamberlain's Men? What's he going to do when he sees us at the Globe? He'll point us out! Is that what you want?"

My mind was in a whirl at this. Why were these men going to be at the Globe?

The younger man looked at me, sighed, and then said quietly, "No."

"Then do what you have to do."

With that, the bearded man strode to the door andm went out.

I looked at the younger man, appealing to his better nature.

"Please!" I begged him. "I meant no harm. I *am* an actor. You can check. Ask anyone in the Chamberlain's Men! Ask Richard Burbage! Ask William Shakespeare! I messed up getting a skull for the next production…"

"Quiet!" said the man.

From his belt he produced a long knife, its blade glinting in the light of the candle on the table.

"I don't want to kill you, but I am a soldier," he stated. "As a soldier I follow orders."

"Why?!" I howled. "I haven't done anything!"

I backed away from him as he came nearer, the light from the candle now flickering and throwing my shadow onto him as I backed towards the table, making him look even more terrifying.

"Please!" I begged.

"I'm sorry," he said.

With that he drew back the knife, ready to strike. Frantically I whirled around, snatched up the candle from the table, and thrust it into his face. The flames caught him in the eyes and he dropped the knife with a howl of pain.

I didn't wait for the thugs outside the door to come in. I rushed to a small opening I'd spotted in the back wall, one that must lead into the alley that ran at the back of Cripplegate.

The next second I was running down the alley. Behind me I could hear yells and shouts from the tavern. The thugs had obviously burst into the back room on hearing the young man's screams. I reached the end of the alley and as I ran out from it, a hand grabbed me and hauled me back.

"Help!" I yelled.

"Quiet!" hissed a voice.

It was Shakespeare.

"I found the man!" I burst out.

"I'd hoped you would," he said. "Tell me all!"

I described the men as clearly as I could. It wasn't too difficult. My memory of the man who'd given orders to have me killed was especially vivid.

"He said I had to be killed, because I'd point them out when they came to the Globe."

"The Globe!"

Shakespeare clapped his hands together and let out a cry of realization.

"Of course!" he said. "That's when they plan to carry out their scheme, at the performance of my new play, with the queen in gracious attendance! She'll be in public view, with every Tom, Dick and Harry able to get within a crossbow's length of her." Turning to me, he said fiercely: "Henry, it's up to you and I to stop this happening!"

"How?" I asked.

Shakespeare frowned thoughtfully.

"I'll think of something," he said.

Whether he did think of something or not, I didn't find out; he vanished. This wasn't that unusual; when one of his plays was about to go on, he often stayed away from the theatre. Most of us thought he was keeping out of Burbage's way, in case B urbage tried to get him to write new stuff at short notice. That was something he had done before. But in this case it was unusual because Shakespeare was also supposed to be acting a part in the play. When the day of the first performance arrived and there was still no sign of Shakespeare, there was uproar behind the scenes at the Globe.

"I bet it's some woman he's got mixed up with," sighed Armin. "Remember, he disappeared for days when we were putting on *Measure for Measure*."

"But he still turned up for the actual performance," said Burbage. "Come on, one of you must know where Shakespeare is!"

I was wondering whether I ought to say something about Shakespeare and the plot to kill the queen – maybe Shakespeare had been killed by one of the assassins! – when a voice from the rear entrance called out: "Did I hear someone say they were looking for Will Shakespeare?"

We all turned to look at the person who had spoken. He was a gentleman. At least, his dress suggested that he came from a fine family.

"And who might you be, sir?" asked Burbage.

"Robert Fitzgerald, at your service," said Fitzgerald, with a bow. "Actor and musician, with a message from your friend, Shakespeare. He begs your pardon but he is afraid that he is indisposed and will be unable to appear on stage."

"Indisposed?!" gasped Burbage, shocked. "Doesn't he realize the queen is coming today?!"

"He does, and for that reason he has asked me to step into his shoes, with your kind permission."

Burbage swore loudly, and then said: "I don't care whose kind permission you crave, sir, you can't just walk on stage and appear in a play without knowing the part!"

"Oh, I know the part, Master Burbage," said Fitzgerald. "Master Shakespeare gave me his own copy of the play for me to study and learn. I have it here."

And with that Fitzgerald produced from his pouch a sheaf of papers which we all recognized as a copy of *The Taming of the Shrew*.

"Fine!" said Burbage. "Then go and get changed. Henry, show our new actor friend where the dressing room is, and explain to him the ways of our theatre. We'll talk later about the reasons for Master Shakespeare's indisposition. Right now, we have a play to prepare!"

As the other actors went about their business, preparing themselves, their make-up, their costumes and their props, our new actor came towards me, a smile on his face.

"Henry," he said. "Master Burbage says you will show me around and help this poor new actor."

I looked at him coldly.

"I'd be more likely to believe you were a poor new actor if you hadn't recognized me without us being introduced," I said.

The smile was wiped off his face for a moment. Then he smiled again, but this time without humour.

"Clever," he said. "Yes, I made a mistake there. Well spotted."

"I know who you are and why you're here," I said boldly. "I shall inform on you and have you arrested."

"On what charge?" said Fitzgerald, and he still smiled. "What evidence do you have? None. Especially without your friend Shakespeare to support you."

"I'll tell them you plan to assassinate the queen," I said. "Then they'll arrest you."

"And I shall laugh and ask how anyone can assassinate the queen when they're on stage!"

"You won't be on stage all the time," I countered.

"True," he said. "But who do you think they will believe? You, a guttersnipe, a mere boy, or me, a gentleman, an actor, and a friend of Will Shakespeare?"

"You are no friend of Shakespeare's!" I retorted. "What have you done with him?"

Fitzgerald laughed.

"I?" he smiled. "*I* have done nothing with him."

"I know who you are," I said again. "And I will stop you."

Fitzgerald stopped smiling. He bent down and put his face close to mine.

"I could kill you now, boy, and no one would care a fig. It would be an accident. But I will let you live, for the moment, because it suits me. You can do nothing to me. You have no evidence. You have no one to turn to, other than Shakespeare. You have no names you can call for help. Stay out of this, boy, and I may let you live. Interfere, and you will die immediately. And don't think about running off and trying to stop me. If that happens, I have friends who will come for you. We know where you live. We know everything about you. I've been paid to kill you, and I will. I'll either do it today, or I'll do it tomorrow."

With that he stood up straight again, and resumed his smile.

"Now, will you show me the dressing room?"

My mind was in a whirl as I showed Fitzgerald to the dressing room. What could I do? Who could I tell? Fitzgerald was right, no one would believe me, not until after it was over and the queen was dead, and then it would be too late.

Fitzgerald had to be stopped, but how? My only ally, Shakespeare, had disappeared. And even if I tried telling someone like Burbage, no one would believe me. Look how Armin had reacted when I'd mentioned those words, "The queen must die."

Thinking about Armin put an idea into my head – an idea involving his dog, Fido. Suddenly, I realized I had a way to stop Fitzgerald killing me, and maybe to stop the assassination, too. But I needed meat.

I slipped out and made for Peters' Butcher's Shop, just around the corner from the Globe. When I got back, with some offal stuffed inside my jerkin, I bumped into Armin and Fido. Fido perked up and started leaping up at me, his nostrils having smelt out the meat, but I pushed him down.

"Ah, there you are," said Armin. "The new man, Fitzgerald, was looking for you."

"Why?" I asked suspiciously.

"To rehearse your duel scene."

"What duel scene?" I asked, puzzled.

"You'd know if you hadn't run off. That copy of the play he brought in has a new piece of business Shakespeare's added. A duel scene – he challenges you to a sword fight."

I felt an icy chill run up my spine.

"Who wins?" I asked.

"He does, of course!" snorted Armin. "After all, he's an actor, you're only an extra! Anyway, you ought to be delighted. You get to perform a duel in front of the queen! A special honour! Even if you do get killed."

"I can't fight a duel," I protested. "I've never used a sword!"

"Too bad," said Armin. "Burbage thought it was a great idea."

Cursing myself for an idiot I hurried back to the props room and came face to face with Fitzgerald, who was practising thrusts and parries with a prop sword.

"I won't fight you," I said simply.

Fitzgerald turned and smiled at me.

"Ah, there you are!" he said. "I wondered where you'd got to."

"I won't fight you," I said again.

"Oh, I think you will," he said. "Because my job is to kill you. Now, I can do it here and now, or I can do it after the play. Or, we can do it this way, when you have a fighting chance."

He was going to enjoy killing me. What's more, he was going to do it in front of two thousand people, and the queen and her entourage, and get away with it by blaming my death on a prop sword that "accidentally" lost its protective tip. And *I* would get the blame for that, after my death, because I was in charge of all the props.

"I'll run away," I said. "Before the fight scene."

Fitzgerald shook his head.

"Remember, what I said," he grinned. "We know where you live! You can't escape!"

Fitzgerald picked out a sword and tossed it towards me. I fumbled for it but managed to catch it.

"We have an hour before the play begins," said Fitzgerald, with that same mad smile. "I'd get some practice in, if I were you."

Actually, I didn't get much chance to practise, because the doors of the theatre opened and the audience poured in. Those with twopenny tickets for seats crammed into the galleries. The inns-of-court men and the lawyers and their women took possession of their boxes, with their private rooms behind them. The groundlings, those who paid just a penny to stand and watch the play from the pit, jostled to get positions at the front near the stage.

A great cheer went up as the queen and her entourage, her ladies-in-waiting, bodyguards and other cronies from Court, took their places in the Nobles' Gallery. As I looked up at her I wondered if those surrounding her were conspirators who meant to assassinate her.

There was no time for me to think any further, because Burbage appeared behind me and grabbed me by the shoulder.

"Right, Henry!" he ordered. "Stop standing around gawking! We have a Royal Command performance to put on! Let the play begin!"

And so the first ever performance of Shakespeare's *The Taming of the Shrew* got under way. It had a very complicated plot, but that was Shakespeare's style. I told him once that he made his plots too confusing, but he just clipped me round the ear and said the world was already too full of critics and it didn't need another one.

The first two acts passed quite smoothly. Fido, as well-behaved as ever, sat by the side of the stage like the obedient dog he was, and watched. I just hoped he wouldn't be too obedient later on...

All too soon it was time for me to go on. I stood at one side of the stage and watched as Fitzgerald went into action, strutting around the stage, delivering his lines and flashing his sword. I had to admit, he cut a fine figure. The audience loved him. He looked suitably villainous but at the same time handsome and dashing.

I felt my hands grip the hilt of my prop sword as Fitzgerald launched into the speech he'd written for himself, the one he'd claimed was added by Shakespeare to lead into our duel.

"But yet there is one among you who I feareth dost call me liar by his look!"

And at that he turned and pointed his sword at me. "I call you villain!"

There was a stirring of interest from the crowd. Up till now there'd just been words and words and more words, no comic business, no fighting, nothing to grab their attention. Now it looked as if all that was about to change.

"Indeed, sire!" I retorted. "But I call thee villain and foul murderer!"

And I flourished my sword.

"Then have at you!" shouted Fitzgerald joyously, and with that he launched himself at me.

The crowd cheered. At last, some action! This was what they'd paid their money for!

Luckily for me, Fitzgerald was so confident of winning that he decided to enjoy it and have fun at my expense, giving the audience their money's worth of spectacle at the same time. His blade flashed and whirled as it went past my head on either side, just missing me. On either stroke he could have cut my ears off, if he'd wished.

I did my best to ward off his thrusts with my sword, but it was no good, and I soon decided retreat was my best policy. Actually, "retreat" was an understatement. I turned and ran, round and round the stage. Fitzgerald gave chase after me. The audience cheered.

Fitzgerald scowled, annoyed. His great moment was being turned into slapstick comedy.

"Stay still!" he snarled at me under his breath.

I kept running. The audience roared with laughter and whistled.

Fitzgerald was now looking furious. He stopped running after me and turned to face me, sword ready to run me through, on my next circuit of the stage. Instead, I skidded to a stop.

The audience roared and clapped. There were shouts of "Go for him!"

Fitzgerald decided to do just that. He levelled his sword at my chest. I could tell by the grim expression on his face that he'd had enough of this, and now he was going to kill me. It was at that point I reached into my jerkin and pulled out a piece of raw meat.

"Here, Fido!" I shouted, and I threw it straight at Fitzgerald. Still sticky with blood, it stuck to his costume. Fitzgerald gaped down at it, bewildered.

"Food, Fido!" I yelled desperately, and I took another piece of meat from inside my jerkin and threw that at Fitzgerald.

The crowd roared with laughter at the sight of Fitzgerald standing there with pieces of raw meat clinging to him.

"Fido!" I called again, more urgently this time. And now the crowd took up the call, urging their favourite to appear. "Fido! Fido! Fido!" they chanted.

Whether it was the familiar sound of laughter, or his name being called so loudly, or the smell of raw meat to a hungry dog, I don't know, but Fido suddenly gave in and rushed onto the stage and leaped up at Fitzgerald and the meat.

There was a huge uproar from the crowd, whistling and cheering and guffaws of laughter as Fitzgerald tried in vain to push the dog away – Fido kept jumping up.

From the other side of the stage Burbage came storming over to me and demanded in a whisper, "What do you think you're doing! You're ruining the play!"

"I'll explain later," I said.

At the side of the stage I could see the prompter going mad, turning over the pages of his play script and trying to work out where we were.

"I'm being upstaged by a dog!" hissed Burbage through gritted teeth. "I'll kill you for this!"

Not if Fitzgerald kills me first, I thought grimly.

A roar of delight from the crowd made me turn to see what was happening. Fitzgerald was now in trouble. In trying to get away from the jumping Fido, he'd tripped over and was now lying on the stage, Fido standing on top of him with all four legs on his chest, chewing the meat.

I wasted no time. I rushed over and trod hard on Fitzgerald's fingers. He let out a cry of pain and let the sword go.

I snatched it up and then levelled it at him, the point right at his throat. Now there was sudden fear in his eyes. All I had to do was push the sharp point in through the soft tissue of his skin, and he was dead.

"Now, varlet!" I roared. "Let me relate to this audience the foul plot thou hast been involved in. A plot to murder no less a wondrous person than our own dear queen!"

"What are you doing?!" whispered Burbage. "This isn't in the script! There isn't any plot against the queen in *The Shrew*!"

"Wilt thou confess, villain!" I shouted at the fallen Fitzgerald. "Wilt thou confess thy part in the plot to commit murder most foul, before all these people, or wilt thou die at my hand?!"

It had seemed to me so obvious that at this point Fitzgerald would start confessing all, the guards would rush in and arrest everyone he named as part of the plot, and the queen would be saved. That's certainly what I would have done in the same circumstances. Instead, to my horror, the fear went from Fitzgerald's face, and a sort of calm came over it. He looked up at me, and then shouted: "Nay! I will confess nothing! Kill me and have done with it!"

I was trapped.

I stood helplessly, wondering what to do next, with two thousand people watching me all agog, also wondering what my next move would be, when from above me where the royal party were sitting, a voice called: "Well done!"

Everyone looked up, and a gasp went through the theatre as one of the queen's ladies-in-waiting suddenly tore off her headdress and veil to reveal the face of none other than William Shakespeare himself.

"Burbage and you others!" called Shakespeare. "Hold that villain! He *is* an assassin!"

Immediately Burbage and Armin came rushing forward to grab hold of me, stopping only as Shakespeare shouted out: "Not Henry! The one with the dog on him!"

Fitzgerald, recovering himself, had been trying to scramble to his feet during all this, but was having difficulty due to the fact that Fido was still trying to lick parts of his costume. Burbage took no chances. He gave one of his famous kicks at Fitzgerald and sent him tumbling back down onto the stage floor. Then he and the other actors leapt upon the fallen man, while Armin tried to rescue Fido from the scrum.

Meanwhile a gasp of horror from the crowd told me that something was happening up in the Nobles' Gallery above. I looked up to see Shakespeare grappling with one of the queen's bodyguards, a huge burly man who was wielding a knife.

I looked towards the rest of the royal party. The queen sat there and just watched as Shakespeare and the bodyguard struggled, her face an impassive mask of white make-up. In her position I would have been running for cover. Not Queen Elizabeth. She sat there as if this struggle with an assassin who had been hired to kill her was a mere inconvenience.

Then one of the men in the box with her, a tall bearded man, stood up and stepped past her, taking out a dagger as he did so. He reached

Shakespeare and the bodyguard, just as Shakespeare wrenched the knife out of the bodyguard's hand. Before anyone realized what was happening, the tall man thrust his dagger hard between the shoulder blades of the bodyguard-assassin. The man gave a cry that turned into a choking noise, and then fell to the floor.

The queen turned to the tall man as he wiped his dagger and put it back into its sheath.

"Thank you, Lord Walsingham," she said brusquely. "Pray remove the body."

Then she turned to the audience and the actors gaping up at her and said coolly, "Perhaps now we can continue with the play."

1587–1605

The struggle for power between the Catholic and Protestant branches of the Christian religion continued. After Elizabeth died without an heir, James VI of Scotland, the son of Elizabeth's Catholic cousin, Mary Queen of Scots, became King James I of England. James had been brought up as a Protestant, but he was keen to encourage religious freedom in England. Unfortunately for James, this attitude annoyed the hard-line Protestant English Parliamentarians, who thought he was favouring Catholics, and also upset hard-line Catholics, who wanted a Catholic monarch on the English throne.

In 1605, things came to a head…

The Gunpowder Plot 1605

"Jenny! Pay attention to your stitches and stop dreaming!"

"I wasn't dreaming, aunt!" protested Jenny.

"Yes you were! I know that look on your face! If you dream you'll make a mess of the stitching and the customer will refuse to pay for the work! It's hard enough getting the gentry to pay as it is."

Jenny Baker sighed and turned her attention to the needlework on the shirt she was making. At times like this, with her aunt nagging her, and her fingers smarting from where she'd pricked her fingers with the sharp point of the needle, she wondered if she'd made the right choice. When her Aunt Maud had offered her a place at her sewing shop, making and mending clothes, Jenny had jumped at the chance. She knew it was either that, or work for her father in his bakery, and she'd hated the idea of all that flour getting in her hair and on her clothes, and the smell of the dough when the yeast was working, making her feel sick. But this sewing, although cleaner than working in a bakery, was hard work. And her Aunt Maud watched her and the two other girls in the shop, Edith and Lizzie, like a hawk. Any stitching that Aunt Maud considered to be badly done had to be unpicked and done again – and again and again, until Aunt Maud was satisfied.

But then, Jenny had to admit, it was true what her aunt said about the gentry not wanting to pay and using every excuse to avoid actually handing over their money for the work done. Although the gentleman that Jenny was making the shirt for, Master Fawkes, seemed nice enough. He was a man in his thirties, Jenny thought, and with such a dark complexion that at first she thought he must be a foreigner. But then, when he spoke, he had an accent that came from northern England. Jenny recognized it because many of the shop's customers seemed to come from the north, Yorkshire or Lancashire, and even from Scotland.

Jenny was bent over her task, her needle and thread nipping through the blue material, when a shadow fell over her. *Not my aunt again*, she groaned inwardly. But the voice that she heard was a man's.

"And how's my shirt coming on, young lass?" he asked.

Jenny recognized the voice and she looked up into the smiling face of that very man she'd just been thinking about, Guy Fawkes.

"Er … very well, sir," Jenny stammered.

She was taken by surprise because usually she didn't get to talk to the customers. They came in and talked with her aunt about their requirements, and prices, while Jenny, Edith and Lizzie sewed and watched and listened.

"Mr Fawkes!" Aunt Maud appeared beside them, obviously flustered. After telling Jenny off, she must have nipped out of the shop for some reason, unnoticed by Jenny, and had returned to find one of her valued customers in conversation with her niece, a lowly worker.

"Ah, Mistress Baker," smiled Fawkes. "I was in the area so I thought I'd call in and see how my new clothes were coming on."

"Very well indeed," said Aunt Maud, recovering her composure. She gestured towards Edith and Lizzie. "Lizzie and Edith are hard at work on your jerkin, and Jenny here – as you can see – is making a very good job of your shirt."

Very good, thought Jenny sourly. That's not what her aunt said when she was talking to *Jenny* about her sewing. Then she used words like *slipshod* and *slack* and *careless*.

"Mistress Baker!"

Another voice, this time a woman who had just come into the shop. Jenny recognized her as Mrs Wharton, a woman who her aunt always had difficulty getting money out of. Mrs Wharton was always bringing her clothes back and complaining that this stitch wasn't right, or this shade of cloth was wrong despite the fact that everyone in the shop knew the work was perfect and exactly as Mrs Wharton had ordered.

Mrs Wharton was holding a cloak she'd recently had made and looking particularly offended. Jenny was glad that it had been Lizzie who'd done the work on the cloak and not her.

"If you'll excuse me, Mr Fawkes," said Aunt Maud with an apologetic smile. "I'll just deal with Mrs Wharton and then I'll be with you."

Guy Fawkes nodded.

"No problem, Mistress Baker, I can entertain myself watching the girls work and admiring the dexterity of their fingers."

Jenny lowered her head, but she couldn't resist looking at Lizzie and Edith, and the three girls exchanged smiles of pleasure at the compliment. Compliments were very rare in Aunt Maud's shop.

As Aunt Maud engaged Mrs Wharton, and began to inspect the places on the cloak the dissatisfied customer pointed at, Jenny noticed another man enter the shop. She hadn't seen this man before, and he didn't seem interested in examining the rolls of cloth on display, like the usual prospective customers. Instead, he walked straight to Mr Fawkes and began to whisper in urgent tones, "Guy, your landlady said I'd find you here."

"Calm down, Robert," said Fawkes. "What's so urgent?"

"What is urgent is that we may well be discovered," hissed the man called Robert. "Everything is in place, but there is talk of guards inspecting Parliament, and if they go into the undercroft…"

"Hush!" commanded Fawkes, and he shot a concerned glance towards Jenny. But Jenny kept her head down and pretended to concentrate on her sewing, while her ears strained to catch the conversation between the two men. But that conversation had ceased. Instead, Fawkes called to Aunt Maud, "Mistress Baker, please accept my apologies, but I have to take my leave of you. I shall return tomorrow, if that suits you."

"It will be my pleasure, Mr Fawkes," said Aunt Maud. Jenny could tell from her aunt's expression that she would much rather have been talking to the nice Mr Fawkes than the dreaded Mrs Wharton, but a customer is a customer.

As Fawkes and the man called Robert left the shop, Jenny's mind was in a whirl. Why had the man seemed frightened? What was it that he feared had "been discovered"? And why was he worried about the guards going into the undercroft of Parliament? For that matter, where was the undercroft? Jenny knew that in large churches, the undercroft meant the large cellars where things were stored, so she assumed there must be an undercroft at Parliament, too. But what was in there that Robert was so scared of the guards discovering?

That night, after Aunt Maud had closed the shop and the girls had had their supper and gone to the tiny attic room they shared above the shop, Jenny told Lizzie and Edith what she'd heard. They looked back at her, puzzled.

"What are you saying, Jenny?" asked Edith.

Jenny felt exasperated. It was so obvious what she was saying.

"That Mr Guy Fawkes and this Robert man are up to something, and it involves the undercroft beneath Parliament. There's something there they don't want the guards to find."

Lizzie laughed.

"Oh Jenny, you and your imagination!" she laughed.

"What do you mean?" demanded Jenny indignantly.

"They're just two men talking men's business," said Lizzie.

"Lizzie's right," nodded Edith. "And they're both gentlemen. Those kind of gentlemen don't get up to bad things."

"That's right," said Lizzie, then she chuckled again. "They get other people to do it for them."

Jenny stared at the two girls, furious with them.

"How can you just ignore it?" she demanded hotly. "There's something going on, and I have to tell someone..."

"No, you don't," said Lizzie firmly, and now she wasn't laughing. "They are gentry going about their business. If you start talking about them to anyone and something bad happens to them, after it's all over you and your aunt will get the blame. And then they'll close this place down and we'll be out of work."

Edith thought this over, then nodded in agreement.

"Lizzie's right," she said. "You can't go around accusing gentlemen of things, especially when you don't know what those things are."

"It could be to do with sweethearts," pointed out Lizzie. "Maybe Mr Fawkes is planning to elope with the woman he loves, and this Robert gentleman is helping him do it."

"And that's why Mr Fawkes needs a new shirt and jerkin," agreed Edith. "For his wedding."

"But why mention Parliament?" persisted Jenny. "And the undercroft?"

"Perhaps the woman he loves is the daughter of a man who works in Parliament," said Edith thoughtfully. "And they've got everything hidden there for their getaway, and now it looks as if they might be discovered."

"Exactly," nodded Lizzie. "That's more likely than them being up to something bad."

But Jenny wasn't convinced, and that night as she lay on her mattress, she couldn't sleep for thinking about it. Something was wrong, she was sure. And she was also sure it was nothing to do with eloping or being in love. The only way to find out what was going on was to get into the undercroft in some way and look for herself. But how? The Parliament buildings were well guarded, she couldn't just walk up to one of the guards and say she'd like to look round. She could always go to Parliament and tell the guards she suspected something bad was going to happen, but if she did that, they'd want to know more details. And if she gave them Mr Fawkes's name and it turned out he was innocent, she would suffer very badly indeed for making a false accusation against a member of the gentry.

The next morning, Jenny's mind was still in turmoil as she got up and had breakfast with Aunt Maud and Lizzie and Edith. She considered telling Aunt Maud, but she knew that the expressions of disbelief she'd got the previous night from Lizzie and Edith would pale against the shouting and rage she'd get from her aunt if she confessed her fears.

She settled down to work on Mr Fawkes's shirt, and did her best to concentrate on her stitches, but her mind was so busy thinking about Fawkes and the man called Robert that twice she had to unpick her sewing and redo it.

It was mid-morning that it happened, the event that Jenny ever afterwards thought of as Fate itself intervening.

"Does anyone know where Jeb is?" Aunt Maud demanded suddenly.

Jenny, Lizzie and Edith looked at one another and shook their heads.

Jeb was a boy who did the heavy work for her aunt at the shop, and also ran errands, including delivering clothes to customers.

"That lazy boy!" raged Aunt Maud. "Today of all days he lets me down!"

Actually, Jenny thought that Jeb often let her aunt down. That was because he *was* lazy. But he was also cheap, and Aunt Maud didn't like spending any more money than she had to. It was for that reason that she often overlooked the fact that Jeb was late for work, or sometimes – like today – didn't turn up at all. Someone who was regular and reliable would also ask for regular and better wages than Jeb.

"I have to get this cloak to the Sergeant-at-Arms at Parliament!" She patted a cloak that Lizzie had recently repaired, and which was now folded up on a table. "He needs it today because tomorrow is the official opening of the new Parliament!"

"I'll take it for you, aunt!" offered Jenny, standing up quickly.

Aunt Maud looked at Jenny suspiciously. Her niece didn't usually volunteer to do anything.

"You?" she asked, warily.

Jenny nodded.

"I know my way there," she said, "and I can be there and back quickly. Certainly as quickly as Jeb."

Her aunt would know that much would be true. Jeb liked to saunter and take his time when he did a delivery.

Aunt Maud frowned with the agony of indecision, torn between losing the valuable time Jenny would be working with her needle, and getting the cloak to the Sergeant-at-Arms. True, she could call out for someone in the street to take it, but they would ask for money, and there was no trusting that they might not sell the cloak to someone on the way.

"Very well," she said. She wrapped the freshly repaired cloak in paper and tied it with string, then handed the bundle to Jenny. "But you are to give it to no one but the Sergeant-at-Arms himself. Is that understood? Some of these soldiers are rogues who would sell their grandmother for a penny. They are not to be trusted."

"I understand, aunt," nodded Jenny. As she left the shop, she heard her aunt's words ringing in her ears: "And don't take too long! There is work to do here!"

Jenny hurried through the crowded streets to Westminster and the two buildings of the large Palace of Westminster that housed both Houses of Parliament, the House of Lords and the House of Commons. She guessed that both Houses had an undercroft, but which one had Guy Fawkes and Robert been talking about? And how was she going to get into either of them?

Please let there be a way! she prayed silently. *Please let the Sergeant-at-Arms be in one of the undercrofts so that I have to be sent down to him.*

But her prayers weren't answered. She reached the imposing doorway of the House of Commons.

"I am come from Mistress Baker the seamstress," she told the soldier on duty at the door. "I have a parcel needed most urgently for the Sergeant-at-Arms."

"Leave it here," said the soldier. "I'll see that he gets it."

Jenny shook her head.

"Mistress Baker says I am to place it into his own hands," she said.

The soldier looked at Jenny, and at the parcel in her arms, suspiciously.

"Why?" he asked.

Because she thinks you are all thieves and rogues, thought Jenny. Instead, she said, "Because he told her to make sure that happened. He said it was to only be given to him."

The soldier looked at her, as suspicious as before, then gestured inside.

"He's inside with the guard," he told her. "But don't interrupt him if he's drilling them. He won't thank you for it."

"Thank you," said Jenny, and she hurried in through the doorway.

Inside, the building was the most magnificent she'd ever seen. The walls weren't brick or stone, they were panelled with wood, and each panel had been painted with a different picture. Some were landscapes, trees and flowers, with deer racing. Some were sea scenes, with ships. Others were fine full-length portraits. And each picture was adorned with gold: here brightening a costume, or there showing sunlight on a leaf.

Jenny remembered that this place had been a royal palace before it became the Houses of Parliament, and inside it still looked like one.

As she ventured in, almost afraid to breathe out in case she damaged any of the wonderful furnishings, she heard the sound of a raised voice shouting instructions and the stamp of boots. She guessed the

Sergeant-at-Arms was putting the guards through their paces – drilling them, as the guard at the door had said – and so was not to be disturbed. In which case, this could be her opportunity. If she could find the undercroft...

It was then that she saw the open doorway to one side, and the stone steps leading downwards.

She checked to make sure that no one was watching her, and then she hurried to the side door and rushed through. At the top of the stone steps she stopped and listened, in case there was anyone down below in the cellar area, but all seemed quiet. Cautiously she went down the steps, moving as quietly as she could.

If I'm stopped and asked what I'm doing, I'll say I was looking for the Sergeant-at-Arms, she told herself.

She reached the bottom of the steps, and the smell of damp earth came to her nostrils. This was it: the cellars, the undercroft. What was down here that so worried that man, Robert?

Suddenly the thought struck her that there may be someone hidden down here, perhaps a prisoner, chained up and left to die. Possibly on the orders of the King. If that was the case and she found him or her, then what would happen to her? They would have to kill Jenny to silence her.

At that thought, she almost turned around and went back up the stairs. But then she stood there, the parcel clutched to her, and strained her ears for any kind of sound. None came, except the squeaks and rustles of rats and mice. Rats and mice, the two creatures it was impossible to get away from in London. They were everywhere, and especially in cellars and underground places.

Slowly, carefully, Jenny ventured into the undercroft. It was dim, but here and there light came through from small windows set high up in the walls, and in the gaps of the wooden floorboards of the floors above. She moved further into the large cellar, keeping away from the walls and supporting columns of stone, in case someone should be hiding there. Or some *thing*. Who knew what horrible thing might not be kept down here?

She carried on walking, slowly, the earth damp beneath her feet, a smell of mould in the air.

There were thick cobwebs, decorating the upper parts of the stone columns and the roof beams and the tops of the walls, but there was nothing else. The undercroft was empty.

They meant nothing, Jenny said to herself. *It was just innocent talk.*

On one level she felt relieved, especially that she hadn't said anything and so wouldn't get into trouble. But a big part of her felt disappointed. She had been so *sure* that something bad was down here, and there was some terrible plot going on, and that Mr Fawkes and the man called Robert were part of it.

She was just about to turn and walk back to the stone steps, when she saw what looked like a recess in the far wall. Curious, she moved towards it, and as she neared it she realized that it was the entrance to what seemed to be a tunnel.

The tunnel was long and dark, but at the far end there was a dim glow. Jenny hesitated, and then moved forward. The tunnel was low; her head almost touched the roof. The tunnel seemed to have been carved directly out of the soil. At intervals wooden struts had been hammered into place to support the roof.

She moved slowly, listening all the while. Finally, she arrived at the far end, and stepped out into a cellar every bit as big as the undercroft she had just left.

This must be under the other House, she realized, the House of Lords. And there, in the middle of the cellar, were stacked barrels of something. She moved towards them. What was in them? Maybe sugar, or grain? Perhaps this was where the food for the House of Lords was stored, but it didn't make sense to keep food stores where it was so damp, and where rats and mice were in such abundance.

She reached the barrels and tapped on the nearest one. It was full. As was the next. And the next.

Then she saw, dangling down from a small hole in the side of one of the barrels, a piece of tarred string. It looked like a fuse, the sort she'd seen on the cannon placed around the city.

Suddenly, with a feeling of horror that struck deep inside her, she realized what was in the barrels. The only thing that would need a fuse. It was gunpowder. And this was the plot. Tomorrow Parliament would open for its next round of sessions; the ceremony attended by the Lords and the Commons, and opened by the King. Fawkes and Robert, and whoever else was in it with them, planned to blow up the House of Lords and kill the king and everyone else in the building.

There were so many barrels of gunpowder, it must have taken months to bring it here. How had they smuggled it in? Jenny couldn't even begin to guess, but it showed that Fawkes must have a great deal of accomplices. She looked around, searching for a door that would take her back upstairs. There was a door in the corner of the cellar, and Jenny hurried to it. It was locked! Either the guards had locked it, or the plotters were making sure the gunpowder wouldn't be discovered accidentally.

Jenny hurried back to the long dark tunnel, and through it to the empty cellars beneath the House of Commons. She hurried up the stone steps to the wooden door. It was shut. She pulled at the handle, but the door wouldn't give. That door had been locked as well! But who by? Had the plotters returned and locked the door? If so, and she banged and called for help, then it would be the plotters who would hear her and open the door and find her … and kill her.

I have to try, she told herself desperately. *If I just stay here, then tomorrow the plotters will unlock the door and find me and kill me anyway.*

"Help!" Jenny banged on the door. "Help! Help!"

The door was made of solid oak and didn't even budge against the blows from her fists. She wondered if her voice would even be heard through the thick wood of the door.

She banged again at the door, shouting as loudly as she could all the while, and finally she heard the sound of metal on metal from the other side as a key was pushed in, and then turned.

The door swung open and a soldier stood there, looking at her.

"Who are you?" he demanded, stunned.

"I have a cloak for the Sergeant-at-Arms," said Jenny.

"I am the Sergeant-at-Arms," said a voice from behind the soldier.

Jenny looked at the face of the man. A hard face, inscrutable, giving nothing away. Was he part of the plot? And then she remembered what her Aunt Maud had said: he needs the cloak for tomorrow's ceremony. If he was going to be here in Parliament as part of that ceremony, then he wasn't part of the plot.

"There is gunpowder!" she burst out hoarsely.

The Sergeant-at-Arms and the soldier stared at her, bewildered.

"What?" demanded the Sergeant.

"Gunpowder," she said, pointing at the stone steps. "In the other cellar. Through the tunnel."

The Sergeant's eyes narrowed and a hard determined scowl formed on his face.

"Guards!" he called out. "Follow me!" To the soldier who'd unlocked the door, he ordered, "Keep her here till I return."

Then the Sergeant raced down the stone steps to the cellar, a squadron of guards hurrying after him.

The Sergeant-at-Arms returned after about five minutes, and glared at Jenny.

"How did you find it?" he demanded.

"I-I was looking for something," stammered Jenny. "I didn't know what, but I thought there might be something bad hidden down there."

"Why?" asked the Sergeant brusquely.

"I overheard two men saying something in my aunt's shop. I work there as a seamstress." Jenny held out the parcel. "I came here to bring you your cloak."

The Sergeant ignored the parcel.

"Who were these two men?" he demanded.

"One of them is called Guy Fawkes," said Jenny. "I don't know the name of the other, except that he is called Robert."

The Sergeant looked at Jenny thoughtfully, then nodded.

"You have done well," he said, his voice and his manner softening. He reached out and took the parcel from her. "The king will be very grateful to you for your action. As will all of those who will be here tomorrow." He turned to those guards who had returned from the cellar with him. "Smith, Jenkins," he ordered, "escort this young lady here back to her aunt's shop. You will explain that she is under your protection, but neither you nor she is to answer any questions about what you are doing, or why."

"Yes, sir," replied one of the guards crisply.

"Once at the shop, you will hide in the back room." To Jenny he said: "If either of these men come into the shop again, you are just to go about your normal business. Can you do that?"

"Yes," nodded Jenny.

To the two guards, the Sergeant ordered, "You will remain hidden, unless this young lady looks to be in danger from these men. Only then will you reveal yourself. Otherwise, let everything proceed as normal." He gave a grim smile. "That way we shall be ready for them when they appear tomorrow, or possibly tonight, to try to put their plan into action."

For the first time, the Sergeant gave Jenny a proper, friendly, smile.

"You have done well, young lady. And I shall make sure I tell your aunt so, when all this is over." He patted the paper parcel with his cloak inside. "It was indeed a stroke of good fortune that I chose your aunt to repair my cloak." Then he chuckled. "It is fortunate indeed that her services are the cheapest, otherwise I may well have gone to someone else who did not have such an intelligent niece."

1605–1665

The conspirators behind the Gunpowder Plot (including Guy Fawkes and Robert Catesby) were arrested in the undercroft of the House of Lords on 5 November, 1605, by guards lying in wait for them. It is said the authorities were tipped off by an anonymous letter, but it is also possible that someone may have overheard the plotters making their schemes, even just a whisper or two, which aroused suspicion.

After James I died in 1625, his son, Charles, became King. Political arguments about whether the king should be a Protestant or a Catholic now became overshadowed by the question: should there even be a king or queen at all, or should the country be ruled by elected officials? The moving force behind this question was Oliver Cromwell, a staunch Protestant, a virulent anti-Catholic, and anti-monarchist.

Soon Cromwell's anti-royalist campaign had spread across the whole country, and by 1640 the debate had turned into a Civil War between the Royalists who supported Charles I (also known as Cavaliers), and those who supported Cromwell and his Parliamentarians (known as Roundheads).

The Civil War raged from 1642 until 1649 when King Charles I was executed by order of Parliament.

From 1649 until 1653 England was a Commonwealth, with Oliver Cromwell in charge as Protector.

In 1658 Oliver Cromwell died and was succeeded by his son Richard, but Richard Cromwell didn't have the personal authority his father had, and confidence in him – and the Commonwealth – faded. In 1661, Charles I's son, also called Charles, who'd fled into exile after the execution of his father, was invited by Parliament to return to England and take the throne as Charles II.

In London, the return of a king was viewed with suspicion. The authorities in the city had been mainly Parliamentarian followers of Cromwell and were wary that the new king would want revenge on them for the execution of his father.

But ordinary Londoners had a bigger problem to deal with: Plague!

England, like the rest of the world, had been ravaged by bubonic plague for centuries. It was spread by the fleas that lived on rats – although this was not known at the time. The effects of the plague were catastrophic. In 1603 it killed 30,000 people in London alone. In 1625, 33,500 people died in London and the rest of England when the plague returned again.

In 1665, the plague came back once again, this time killing 20 per cent of London's population. It was believed to have been brought from Holland on Dutch trading ships. The first areas to be affected were London's docks, and then St-Giles-in-the-Field, where the poor lived crammed together. It looked as if nothing could stop the spread of plague in the capital.

The Great Fire 1666

My name is John Baker, I'm twelve years old, and I am a baker. I suppose really I'm an apprentice baker – I was sent to work at the bakery of my cousin, Thomas Farriner in Pudding Lane, because my father, James Baker, said he hadn't got enough work for me at our own family bakery in Westminster. He thought it best for me to continue to learn my trade at another place. To be honest, I don't think that was really true. He found work with himself for my older brother, Gethin, and he'd promised a place at our bakery for my younger brother, Simon, when he became of an age to work, so I don't know why he couldn't find work for me. I can only imagine he doesn't think I'll be as good a baker as Gethin or Simon, but I know I'm every bit as good as my brothers.

So, I went to Pudding Lane, which is in the city of London, inside the old Roman walls, and began to work at my cousin's. My job was mixing the flour and water and salt and yeast to turn it into dough, so that my cousin and the other bakers could turn it into bread shapes. Mixing the dough is heavy work because it gets sticky. It's not too bad if you're only making a few loaves, but when you have to make a large amount of dough, the weight of it as it gets thicker and stickier pulls on your arms, and you have to keep lifting it and turning it all the time to stop it getting lumpy. Dough has to have an even texture all the way through if the bread is going to be good.

The area around my cousin's bakery was the most crowded place I had ever seen. Buildings were crammed so close together that the tops of houses almost touched across the streets and lanes. It was no use having windows in the upper parts of one of these houses, because the only thing you could see was the inside of the opposite house.

It also struck me as a very dangerous place because, as well as the fires that kept my cousin's ovens burning, there were so many other buildings around where open fires were vital to the business: smiths, foundries, glaziers, other bakers, all with fires burning and sparks flying, and the buildings and houses made of wood with thatched roofs.

I commented on the dangers of fire to my cousin when I first joined him, but he just laughed at me.

"You don't want to worry about any fire, John," he told me. "Just look how near we are to the river. If a fire starts, we'll soon have water from the Thames to put it out. And, if we can't put it out, the river is always there for our escape, either on the water or over London Bridge."

It was true that the Thames wasn't far away from his bakery, but I had grave doubts if water could be taken from the river as easily as my cousin said. For one thing a whole shanty town had grown up along the banks of the Thames where the poorest people lived in shacks made of tarpaper. This shanty town spread all the way along the river, the flimsy dwellings going up in the narrow spaces between the warehouses and the jetties. And these warehouses were filled with barrels and boxes of tar, pitch, hemp rope and flax, all necessary for the ships that moored there, but all of which could set fire too easily if a lighted candle was knocked over, or a spark from one of the fires of the shanty houses blew into one of the warehouses.

And as for escaping over London Bridge, I thought this would be very unlikely, as the whole of the north side of the Bridge had even more of these shanty buildings set up on it, blocking the way if a crowd tried to escape.

I was also worried by the amount of black gunpowder that seemed to be stored in the area. Not just at the warehouses, but in people's houses. This was left over from the Civil War, when Oliver Cromwell and his troops had fought against the king and his army. After the war was over and Cromwell's army disbanded, most of the men kept their muskets and pistols. After the throne was restored in the person of our King Charles II, a lot of these old soldiers became suspicious and worried in case the Royalists should persecute and attack them, and so they made sure they had ammunition for their firearms, and kept it stored in their houses. There were so many of Cromwell's old soldiers living and working in the city that the place was solid with gunpowder.

"John," my cousin said to me wearily one day, "I'm tired to the bone of you talking about fire breaking out and us all being burnt to death. You should be more scared of catching the plague than of a fire breaking out! In truth, 'tis our fires that keep the plague away from us!"

I had to admit that on the point of the plague, cousin Thomas was right. There had always been fears of plague ever since I was a small boy, but since the middle of last year the epidemic in London had killed so many people everyone was calling it The Great Plague, the worst outbreak there had ever been in London. 50,000 people had died in the city alone in the last twelve months, and the Mayor and the city authorities had ordered that fires be kept burning night and day because the fumes and smoke were said to be the best defence against the disease.

"Either you stop this fretting, John, or I'll have to return you to your father. And I don't think your father will be glad to have you back."

Thomas was right, my father would be very unhappy indeed if I was returned to him – another mouth to feed.

"But because I know your father will be upset with me as well as you if I send you back, and I don't wish to be blamed for arguments within the family," he added, "I'll prove to you there's nothing to worry about."

"How?" I asked, puzzled.

"Tomorrow, once the first breads have come out of the ovens, I'll take you and show you how the city is prepared. Then you won't worry ever again."

The next day, as he had promised, Thomas took me to the nearest church, and showed me ladders, buckets made of leather, axes, and firehooks stored inside the tower. Firehooks are long poles with hooks at the ends.

"If a fire ever breaks out, and there have been some, then these tools will stop it spreading," said Thomas. "The firehooks are for pulling the thatch off a roof, or even sometimes for pulling down a house. If a house catches fire and the building next to it is pulled down, then the fire can't spread."

I nodded. I knew about these tools as we had the same in the church in my own parish. But we didn't have the same press of buildings so close together, and the large number of open fires that there were here in the city, with the blacksmiths and tinsmiths and whitesmiths and foundries, as well as all the bakers and others who were using fire.

Thomas then took me round to the side of the church and showed me what looked like a four-wheeled cart with barrels on it.

"Our fire engine," he said proudly, gesturing at it. "With barrels filled with water. Two strong men can haul it through the streets to wherever the fire is. There's no need to wait for water from the river."

He then marched a bit further along the church wall, until he came to a pipe made of wood that poked out from the wall. It had a plug fixed firmly in it, and when my cousin removed this plug, water spilled out. My cousin immediately pushed the plug back into place.

"This is just one water point," he said. "There are thousands across the city, all supplied with water from a water tower placed at a high point at Cornhill. Trust me, John, if any fire starts, it'll be soon put out. There is no shortage of water to douse it. *Now* do you believe me when I say there's nothing to worry about?"

I looked at him, unhappy and still doubtful.

"I can see that working during the day, when there are loads of people about who might spot the fire when it starts, but what about at night when people are asleep?" I asked.

My cousin scowled at me, then answered wearily, "There are a thousand watchmen who patrol the city at night. If they see any hazard, such as a fire starting, they'll ring their bell and alert the other watchmen, and wake people up. Trust me, John, if there's any sign of fire, it'll be seen and dealt with." Then, doing his best to keep his patience with me, he said: "Now, let's go back to the bakery. The time we lose is money lost, and poor people like us can't afford to lose so much as a halfpenny."

But two days after my cousin had shown me the fire engine, the firehooks and the other fire tools, the worst happened.

It was just after midnight on Sunday 2 September that I was woken by bells ringing and people shouting in panic. Someone was shaking me, and as my eyes opened I saw it was Richard, one of the young bakers I shared the room with.

"Get up!" he screamed. "Fire!"

Immediately I was aware of the acrid stench of smoke hanging in the room, the fumes filling my nostrils and mouth. I began to choke. The rest of the household had already gathered out in the street. The thatched roof of the bakery was on fire, burning red in the night sky, sparks flying away on the wind.

"The oven!" shouted my cousin Thomas. "The oven caught fire!"

But how could the oven catch fire when it was made of clay? And then I realized he must mean the wood that was stored near it as fuel. The wood was as dry as tinder. That summer of 1666 had been so dry for so long that everything was parched and twisted with waiting for rain. If just one spark had jumped from the oven, the wood stored close to it would have burst into flames.

Already neighbours were out, bringing buckets of water and hurling the water at the flames, but it was making little difference. The flames would die down momentarily as the water splashed onto them, and then they would surge up again, even bigger than before, with a thicker and greasier smoke billowing out and choking everyone.

Suddenly the roof of the bakery disappeared with a crash of timbers. The heat from the fire was so intense it drove us all back, but there was nowhere to move. My cousin pointed to the house nearest to us, where a widow, Mrs Twick lived with her five children, all of whom were now out and watching the fire.

"We have to tear that house down!" he shouted.

"No!" shouted back Mrs Twick. "That is our home!"

"It will burn unless we do!" my cousin insisted.

"And where will we live?" demanded Mrs Twick angrily. "I have five children!"

Even as she said it, the flames suddenly moved across from my cousin's burning bakery and licked at the walls and roof of Mrs Twick's house. In the next second her house was burning.

"Where are the firehooks?" called my cousin. "Tear it down!"

"No!" screamed back Mrs Twick desperately. "The fire engine will save us! Where is the fire engine?"

By now the cry of "Fire!" had gone up throughout the city. Everyone was pouring out of their houses, bringing with them as much as they could carry.

Then, through the smoke, men appeared, carrying the firehooks, axes and ladders from the church.

"There!" shouted my cousin, pointing at Mrs Twick's house, which was now engulfed in flames as the fire spread up its walls and over its roof. "Tear it down!"

The men moved towards the house, firehooks poised, but as they did so, one of the walls of the house collapsed, falling outwards into the street. As soon as that happened, the flames leapt inside the house and began to devour the wood of the walls at a speed which was terrifying to watch. Mrs Twick and her five children began screaming and crying.

"Where is the fire engine?!" shouted my cousin desperately.

But the crowd of people trying to escape from the burning buildings was so great, and the streets and lanes were so narrow, that even he must have known there was no chance of the fire engine getting through.

"The river!" he yelled. "Get water from the river!"

There was no chance of that either, because suddenly the wind changed direction towards the south. By now the heat was so intense that the bone-dry wood of the buildings exploded into flames, cutting off the direct route to the river. Then another building near to us burst into flames, the wind lifting burning thatch and showering it down on us. People began to panic. I saw one man catch fire and he began screaming and trying to beat the flames out with his hands. Luckily, someone had a bucket of water to hand and they threw it over him, dousing the flames, but leaving him moaning and crying with pain.

My cousin looked towards his burning bakery, and at the buildings around us now fast catching alight, despair on his face as he saw his livelihood, and his whole life, going up in flames before his eyes.

"Run!" he yelled. "Save your lives!"

It was already happening: people running, screaming and shouting in panic, abandoning everything they had. But which way to run? The streets to the north were clogged with people, desperate to get away. But that way lay the city wall, which meant people could only get out through the gates in the wall, and I knew that would be a battle as panic drove them to fight and claw at one another to get through those gates.

The river lay to the south, which offered water and safety, but already I could see the flames heading southwards fast, and knew they would be catching on to the shanty houses, and the warehouses that ran along the river.

Whichever way I ran I knew I would find myself caught up in the fire as the dry timbers of the houses and their dry roofs burst into flames. The more houses burned, the hotter the flames would become and the faster they'd travel. The fire had to be stopped. If it was left to burn, the whole city could catch fire.

"I'll stay!" I said. "I'll help stop the fire!"

"No, go!" shouted Thomas. "I couldn't face your father if you died."

I hesitated, then he gave me a push towards the migrating crowds. I joined the crowd, but I knew already that I had to stay and help.

As soon as I was out of sight of my cousin, I ran to where a group of men were chopping at the timbers of a nearby house, and pulling at it with the firehooks. They were trying to create a firebreak, a gap between the raging fire and the rest of the houses so that the flames wouldn't cross and continue.

"Let me help!" I called.

Unlike my cousin Thomas, they didn't send me away. They were sweating, their clothes and faces blackened with soot and smoke. The heat from the flames was incredible. I joined one of the men hauling at the roofing timbers of a house with a firehook, taking hold of the long pole with him and tugging as hard as I could, adding my strength to his. Suddenly the wind sprang up ever stronger, flames leaping high around us, sparks flying through the air and landing on the very timbers we were trying to pull down.

"Move away!" called a man with a big black beard, the leader of the gang, urgency in his voice.

We moved back, just in time, because suddenly the dry timbers we had been pulling at began to spark, and then burst into flames.

"Back! Back!" he shouted.

We retreated. This time the gang of men, with me tagging along, moved to some houses much further away from the licking flames. The men didn't seem to notice that I was with them. All their attention was on the task in hand, creating a firebreak to stop the flames spreading.

Other men, and some women, had joined us now, all eager to lend a hand in trying to stop the fire making the damage worse. The air was getting thicker, the smoke stank and made my eyes water. I tore a piece from my shirt and tied it around my face, I saw a barrel of water nearby, and I went and plunged my head into it so that I was soaked through.

More people had joined us now, all eager to fight the flames, but there was not enough water. And what water there was just spat and fizzled when poured onto the burning timbers before the flames roared up again, even higher and stronger than before, making even thicker and blacker smoke.

I spent all that day, the Monday, helping the workers tear down houses, but as soon as we'd made what we thought was a wide enough firebreak, flames lept across the gap, and sparks flew across and landed on the thatched roofs, or embedded themselves in the wooden walls of the nearest buildings, and soon those houses turned into raging infernos.

"We've lost it, lads!" called the man with the black beard, whose name I had discovered was William, as yet another house caught fire, forcing us to run from it before it collapsed and fell on us. "We have to leave the city to burn!"

"We need to find refuge before *we're* burned!" muttered one man.

"The cathedral!" shouted William. "The walls and roof are made of stone! They won't burn! We'll find sanctuary there!"

And so we ran, still holding our fire-fighting tools in case we had need of them, and made our way through the narrow streets towards St Paul's Cathedral. But the fire was ahead of us, fanned by winds that drove it westwards. When we reached the cathedral we saw, to our horror, that wooden scaffolding poles had been fixed to the sides, right up to the roof of the cathedral, so that repairs could be carried out on the old stonework. The workers had gone, abandoning the cathedral. Now we saw flames lick at the wooden scaffolding.

"It'll burn!" muttered one man fearfully.

"It won't burn inside!" insisted William. "The roof has slates on it, not thatch. The fire won't burn slate."

But he didn't move towards the cathedral. Instead, he stayed back and watched as the flames caught on the scaffolding, and began to work their way upwards towards the roof. Once there, they caught on the wooden roof ladders, and soon flames were dancing across the tiles. All this time the flames on the burning scaffolding were heating up the cathedral's stone walls, I could see them starting to glow, like stones in an oven.

Suddenly there was a yell from one of the men. "The lead!" he shouted. "The lead on the roof!"

We looked up, and saw that the lead on the roof that held the tiles in place was melting and was beginning to run down from the roof, the molten metal pouring and splashing onto the flames that licked the walls.

Suddenly, with an enormous crash, the burning scaffolding fell away from the stone walls of the cathedral, smashing down onto the surrounding area in a mass of flames and sparks and smoke.

"Run!" yelled William. "Run for the city gates!"

We ran. Behind us we heard the hissing and spitting of the molten lead as it boiled and bubbled. Then the explosions began as the stones in the walls, heated beyond any temperature they had ever known before, started to crack and split. Small stones flew past us, hissing, smoke cascading from them as they smashed into the ground around us as we ran. It was lucky that many of the buildings nearby hadn't yet caught fire – they gave us protection from the flying, burning stones, but only until they too exploded; the dry timbers burst into flame in the heat.

I ran northwards towards the city wall, desperate now to get away from the inferno. Behind me there was a huge crash and explosion as the roof of St Paul's Cathedral collapsed, and then I became aware of an even greater searing heat at my back as the cathedral burst into a giant mass of flame.

I had to get away.

It was Wednesday before the Great Fire finally burnt itself out. By then I was back at home with my family in Westminster. When I walked back into our family bakery on the Tuesday, my face and clothes black with smoke from the fires, my father was angry with me for not having come home at once; they were sure I must be dead. But when I told him that I had stayed in the city to help fight the flames and stop the fire spreading, he hugged me close and called me a hero.

I didn't feel like a hero. I felt sad that so much of London had been destroyed, and no one had been able to stop it happening, despite the fire engines, the firehooks, the watchmen and the water spouts. It is only now, November 1666, weeks after the fire, that the real extent of the damage is known.

13,500 houses were destroyed in the fire. 87 churches, the Royal Exchange, the Custom House, the Bridewell Palace, the prisons inside the city walls, St Paul's Cathedral, which I saw destroyed with my own eyes, and the three western gates in the city wall: Aldersgate, Newgate and Ludgate. They say they don't know how many people died. Some say it was just six, others say 600, some say 6,000. All I know is that in just a few days, the City of London was destroyed.

1666–1716

Although there had been fires before in London, the city had never known anything as bad as the Great Fire. The heat was so intense that it melted the steel lying ready on the wharves by the river, and this steel had a melting point of 1,250°C-1,480°C (2,300-2,700°F). The iron locks and chains on the great gates in the City Wall also melted. Much of the area inside the old city walls was laid waste.

Following the Great Fire, a new City of London was built, along the same streets and lines as the old destroyed city. But this time the streets were made wider, so that fire engines and emergency workers could take action much faster in the future if fire broke out. There was also a ban on houses being built alongside the Thames, because they had obstructed efforts to draw water from the river. Also, all buildings were to be made of stone and brick, not wood.

Most of the destroyed churches were rebuilt, 50 of them designed by Christopher Wren. The most famous of Wren's new buildings was the new St Paul's Cathedral. This was particularly appropriate, because it had been Christopher Wren – then a little-known architect – who had been in charge of the renovations to the old St Paul's Cathedral at the time of the fire, and his wooden scaffolding that had caught fire.

It has been suggested that the Great Fire of London put an end to the plague, although historians argue about this, some claiming that the plague was already dying out before the fire began. However, the plague was spread by the fleas on rats; and there is no doubt that the Great Fire got rid of most of the city's rat population.

One irony is that the City Corporation didn't know the reason for the spread of plague. One theory blamed cats and dogs for spreading the plague, so a cull of the city's cats and dogs was ordered. As it turned out, this was a very bad decision, as cats and dogs were the very animals that kept the rat population down. After the cull, the rat – and flea – populations increased, and the plague spread even faster.

Following the fire, Charles II commissioned a tall monument, designed by Christopher Wren and Robert Hook, which was erected near the source of the fire in Pudding Lane as a reminder of the Great Fire of London.

Meanwhile, the bitter disputes and suspicions between Protestants and Catholics, which had been going on since the time of Henry VIII, continued.

As we have seen, after the Commonwealth, King Charles II became king of England. After his death, the throne was taken by his younger brother, James. But James II was a Catholic, and the majority of Parliamentarians were anti-Catholic and intent on keeping the throne of England strictly Protestant. So, just three years after James II became King, he was deposed by Parliament and replaced by his Protestant daughter, Mary, and her Dutch husband, William. The former King

James went into exile in Rome.

This led to great resentment amongst many of the Catholic aristocracy – they felt that their true hereditary king had been wrongly overthrown and replaced by a foreign outsider. This resentment built up and took physical form in the Jacobite rebellions, when supporters of the exiled King James fought to return him to the throne. They were called "Jacobites" because "Jacob" was another form of the name "James".

In 1701 the Act of Settlement was passed, preventing any Catholic from becoming king or queen of England.

In 1702 Mary's younger sister, Anne, became queen of England. During her reign, in 1707, the Act of Union united England and Scotland as the United Kingdom.

Queen Anne had eighteen children, none of whom survived beyond eleven years of age. When she died in 1714, Parliament invited the Protestant Elector of Hanover, George, to become King George I of Great Britain and Ireland. The fact that he couldn't speak English was not considered important. What was important was that his ancestry had been traced back to James I through his mother and grandmother – and that he was a Protestant.

To the Catholics of the new United Kingdom, especially the aristocracy of Scotland who supported the return of King James as the rightful heir to the throne, appointing someone who couldn't even speak English was the final insult.

Escape from the Tower of London 1716

"You have been found guilty of treason against His Gracious Majesty, King George I. You will be taken from this House and returned to the Tower of London, where you will be executed. Do you have anything to say to the court before you are removed from this House?"

Thirteen-year-old Anne Baker sat in the public gallery of the House of Lords and looked down at the figure of William Maxwell, Earl of Nithsdale, standing defiantly between two guards. Next to her sat her mistress Mary Maxwell (Lord Nithsdale's twelve-year-old daughter), the Countess of Nithsdale and her maid, Louise.

On either side of Lord Nithsdale and the two guards, rows of Lords and Bishops sat on the wooden benches, which rose upwards from the floor like seats in a theatre. Directly in front of them, on an ornately carved and decorated throne, sat the High Steward of the House of Lords, Lord Cooper. He was dressed in all his finery, with the insignia of his office embroidered on his cloak, and on his head was a long grey wig. Two pikemen stood stiffly to attention on either side of him, their pikes held firmly by their sides, metal blades gleaming.

This was a popular trial: the cream of Scottish and English aristocracy being brought out one after another onto the floor of the House of Lords for attempting to overthrow the king and put a Catholic on the throne in his place. The Earl of Nithsdale, the Earl of Carnwath, Viscount Kenmuir, Baron Nairn, the Earl of Winton, Lord Derwentwater were just a few of those on trial. In all, 75 "prisoners of quality", as they were described, all from Catholic aristocracy, were charged with taking up arms against the king. They had all been taken prisoner at the Battle of Preston when their Jacobite forces had been outnumbered and defeated by the troops of King George.

The verdicts of "guilty" against them all had been a foregone conclusion. These men had planned to remove George from the throne. Their defence at their trial, that they were not guilty of treason because they did not recognize King George as their true sovereign, was a valiant attempt to fight Law with Law, but it had always been doomed to fail. The cold hard fact was the rebels had to be executed. Not just because if they were left alive they might rise up in rebellion again, but as an example to any other potential rebels. The Lords were saying, *King George I of Hanover is the rightful king of England and Great Britain. Neither the Stuart Pretender nor anyone else has a claim to the English throne. If anyone attempts to enforce the claim of any pretender to the throne, that will be treason and treason is punishable by death.*

Anne watched as Lord Nithsdale turned to look slowly along the rows of assembled Lords and Bishops who had just found him guilty of treason, before turning back to face Lord Cooper. There was no mistaking the contempt he felt for the Lords and for the House itself; it was there to see in his hard, cold expression, in his stance, in everything about him.

"Yes, sir," said Lord Nithsdale, his voice firm, his tones ringing out and filling the large hall. "I have plenty to say to this House, and to the people of this nation! First, George of Hanover is no king of this nation! The rightful king is our majesty James Stuart, James III, by royal descent from the Stuarts in a long line from James I—"

"Quiet, sir! I order you to hold your tongue! I will have no traitorous talk in this House!" ordered Lord Cooper.

"—himself a descendant of Queen Elizabeth of England," continued Maxwell firmly, his voice rising higher as angry shouts and raised voices among the rows of Lords and Peers attempted to drown him out. "This George is no king of England. He cannot even speak English! First we have some Dutchman foisted on us, now we have this German—"

"Silence him! Take him down!" shouted the High Steward angrily.

"—while our own true king exists shamefully in exile—"

Maxwell's words were cut short by one of the guards alongside him pushing a hand over his mouth, while the other grabbed him and began to pull him away from the central floor and towards the door. The countess leapt to her feet.

"Shame on you!" she shouted at Lord Cooper. "He has the right of a nobleman to free speech!"

"No one has the right to air sedition in this House!" the High Steward shouted back, equally angrily. "This House is part of the court of King George and I will hear no talk of rebellion in it. And if you attempt to continue such a traitorous speech, I will have you imprisoned in the Tower alongside your husband, madam!"

The countess hesitated, as if preparing a verbal barb to fire at the High Steward. Then she scowled and pushed her way past the other onlookers in the public gallery. Mary, Anne and Louise got hastily to their feet and hurried after her. Anne guessed that the countess was heading for the stairs that would take them down to the street entrance, where a coach would be waiting to transport the earl and other prisoners to the Tower of London. The people inside the passageways of the House jostled the four as they struggled to push their way through the crowd.

They made it down the stairs and to the entrance out into the street, just as the earl was being pushed onto a coach. Other prisoners were already inside it.

"William!" the countess called, her voice rising above the hubbub of noise in the street.

William Maxwell turned and looked as if he was about to move towards her, but a soldier stepped in front of him and pushed him roughly, forcing him into the coach.

"It will be all right!" Maxwell called to her.

And then the door of the coach was slammed shut.

"What will happen now, Mama?" asked Mary. Anne could tell that Mary was frightened and close to tears, but she was determined not to let them flow. Not in public. Anne had heard the earl tell his daughter: "Be brave, my little one. Don't let our enemies think they have beaten us. We have lost this one battle, but we are strong and we will rise again."

But Anne knew that Mary didn't feel strong. She knew the young girl wanted to rush after the coach as it rattled away over the cobbles and throw herself at the doors, howling and crying, and demand that her father be released. Instead, Anne walked with Mary, and they followed the countess and Louise through the narrow streets of Westminster to a waiting coach.

As the coach made its way through the streets to their house, Anne looked out at the crowds of people going about their business. She had become Mary's maidservant when the Maxwells arrived in London to support the Earl, and in a short time had become fond of the girl, and the Maxwell family. She knew that Mary hated London. Mary had grown up in the countryside of Scotland, in Dumfriesshire. Mary often talked fondly of the place: the countryside, the leafy lanes, and the clean, sweet air. It was a far cry from London with its masses of people, the hundreds and thousands who filled the streets every day, going who knows where to do who knew what, but all in such a hurry.

Anne knew that, to country folk, London was supposed to be glamorous; a place where beautiful ladies and handsomely-dressed men paraded through the drawing rooms of the rich, and at parties, and in the parks. A place where the streets were said to be paved with gold and where all dreams could come true. But for Mary, London was a nightmare rather than a dream. It was dirty and smelt of sewage, rotting vegetables and meat. The smell of horse manure dominated the air from all the coaches and carts and delivery wagons. Mary hated the beggars of all ages and all descriptions crouched in the streets, their hands held out for money. She wanted to go home, back to the hills and open air of Scotland. But she loved her father more than her home country, and Anne knew that Mary wouldn't leave as long as the earl remained a prisoner in London.

Anne had landed the job because the Maxwell family wanted servants who were Catholics, and at this time – with the fear of Catholic rebellion rising throughout Britain – most Catholics preferred to keep their heads down and practise their religion in private. Anne didn't know why her own family were Catholics. She was told that everyone in England had been Catholics before the Tudor King, Henry VIII, had started his own Church, the Church of England. Then many people had switched and become Protestants, some to keep favour with the King, and some because they believed in the new religion. Many of Anne's cousins and relatives were Protestants. She'd asked her mother about it, once, what was the difference.

"Surely we are all Christians?" Anne had asked. "And so we are all the same."

Her mother hadn't been able to answer. She'd then asked her father, who said: "We are poor people. We can't afford to talk about religion. If it suits us, maybe we'll convert to the Anglican Church. But right now, I am what I am, and what my father was."

So her father was a Catholic because he was too busy or idle to change, thought Anne. It didn't seem a very good reason.

But being a Catholic had brought Anne into the employ of the Maxwells. And she wasn't just treated by them as a lowly servant, but with genuine friendship and kindness. It was very different from other friends of hers who worked as maids and were treated harshly by their masters and mistresses.

Father McCree, the family's priest, was waiting at the house for them when they returned. Anne didn't like Father McCree. In her view he was a hypocrite and a coward, happy to verbally attack the king and Protestants loudly, but only when his listeners were staunch Catholics, like the Maxwells. Publicly, he said little. *He didn't even come to the House of Lords today to support the Earl*, thought Anne. He was afraid he might be arrested, though for what, Anne couldn't imagine. Father McCree didn't take up arms in the struggle, like the Earl. No, he bowed down before the king and his court, even though he cursed them in Latin in whispers under his breath.

"How is William?" asked McCree.

"He is defiant," answered the countess.

"Did they find him guilty?"

Mary's mother's face set into a hard and angry look.

"Of course. They will find them all guilty."

McCree shook his head. "The ungodly will rot in hell for what they are doing to God's chosen!" he burst out.

But you'll be safe, crawling to them, thought Anne.

"We should never have attacked Preston so early," said the countess. "My husband advised them that, and so did George Seton, two men who know about warfare. We should have built up our strengths first in Scotland, amassed an army of such strength that the English would have retreated all the way to London. Instead, the English Lords insisted we crossed the border and launched our attack on England too soon." She sighed. "It was a lost cause. An army of just four thousand."

"A cause that will win in the end," said McCree in stirring tones. "I will send an envoy to the Pope and ask for clemency."

The countess gave a mocking laugh.

"Do you think this so-called king will listen to any words from the Pope?" she demanded. She shook her head thoughtfully. "No, there has to be another way to save my husband." And she sank down onto a chair, her face troubled.

Father McCree looked solemn.

"If there is anything I can do, my lady…" he began.

The countess shook her head.

"No, Father. You have done all you can."

"Any spiritual guidance or comfort I can give…" continued the priest.

Again, the countess shook her head.

"I may need such comfort if my husband is executed," she said. "Until them, I need determination to stop that happening."

McCree looked uncomfortable.

"If you are planning anything, my lady, you know as your confessor that anything you tell me is sacrosanct and I would never divulge it," he said fervently. He then added in an awkward voice: "But if I were to be taken and put to torture…"

Or just the threat of torture, thought Anne, doing her best to hide a sneer. She looked at the priest. *You are indeed a coward*, she thought. *Worse, you work men up to rage and anger and urge them to take risks for a cause you say you believe in more than death, but you would not put yourself in any danger.*

"Do not fear, Father. I will not burden you with my thoughts at this stage," said the countess.

The priest nodded.

"But, when it is all over and you wish to make confession…"

"I know that you will be there for me," finished the countess.

And quite likely tell the King's men everything the countess tells you to be sure of saving your own skin, thought Anne.

Louise showed the priest out. When she returned, the countess stood up and turned to Anne.

"Anne, are you loyal to us and our family?" she asked.

The question puzzled Anne.

"Yes, milady," she nodded.

"Yes, she is," added Mary firmly. "When others have sneered at us in the street, Anne has actually challenged them! I do believe she would fight them!"

And I would, thought Anne. She wouldn't let any bully boys attack young Mary. She was her mistress, but also her friend.

The countess stood studying Anne thoughtfully. Then she turned to her maid. "What do you think, Louise?" she asked.

Louise nodded.

"I agree with Mistress Mary that Anne can be trusted."

Trusted with what? thought Anne, her mind in a whirl.

"Very well," said the countess. "Anne, what I am about to say is a secret. So secret that I haven't even discussed it with Mary."

Mary looked at her mother, shocked. "A secret?" she demanded.

The countess nodded, but her eyes were still on Anne.

"Do you swear that once I tell you this secret, you will not tell anyone else?" she asked.

Anne wanted to say, "It depends on what the secret is." But she felt she knew the Maxwells well enough to know that they would not tell her something that might put her in danger. At least, she hoped not.

"I swear," she said, and she made the sign of the cross with her hand.

The countess hesitated, then she said, "We have a plan to help my husband escape from the Tower."

Anne stared at the countess, stunned. Escape from the Tower of London? That was impossible! No one had ever escaped from that terrifying fortress.

Mary looked at her mother, equally shocked.

"How?" Mary demanded. "No one has ever been rescued from the Tower before! All those famous lords and ladies, queens and knights, even those with the largest armies at their call, none ever got out, except for their execution. The Tower is the strongest building in London. No siege could be laid to it, even if we had an army!"

"We don't need an army," said the countess. "All we need are women with strong nerve!"

Mary looked at her mother, as bewildered as Anne. "I don't understand," she said.

The countess gestured to Louise, who walked to the door and looked out into the hallway, and then checked the rooms nearby, before returning.

"There's no one about who can hear us," Louise assured the countess.

Even with this assurance, the countess dropped her voice to a whisper.

"The plan is that the women of the family will visit your father in his cell. We'll all wear many layers of clothes. We'll dress your father in the extra clothes so he looks just like one of the women, with a hood to hide his face. And then we shall walk out. We'll have a coach standing by to take us to the coast, where we'll take a boat to France. The French king will give us his protection. My own view is that we should then travel south to Rome, just in case George sends his assassins after us. We'll be safe in Rome."

Mary stared at her mother, stunned.

"It will never work!" she burst out. "The guards will know him! And they'll count how many women go into the cell and how many come out! They'll see that there's one more!"

"That's what I said," nodded Louise. "That's why I've offered to take his Lordship's place in the cell. Your father and I will change clothes…"

"No!" said the countess firmly. "I will not leave you behind in that filthy place, at the mercy of those guards. At best you will be locked up for helping a prisoner to escape. At worst…" And his words stopped, but there was no mistaking the implication of the threat that lay in store for Louise. "We will all leave. All of us!" Her voice lowered to a whisper again as she told Mary and Anne: "I need at least ten women, all heavily cloaked and hooded, all gathered together in a pack. Too many for the guards to count as we go in the cell, and come out."

"They will not allow that many in," protested Mary.

"They will," said the countess. "The guards there will do anything for money and drink."

"Except let a prisoner escape!" Mary argued.

"We are not asking them to let a prisoner escape," her mother countered. "I will be asking them to let a condemned man see the women of his family and his faithful women servants one last time before he is taken out to die. They will not care about his feelings, or ours. They will see only that we are just women, and therefore not dangerous to them; and that I will pay them in money and drink for their kindness and Christian charity." Her expression hardened and her eyes glittered with determination. "The drink will be strong enough to muddle their senses, just in case they consider counting us as we leave the cell." She hesitated, then said to both Mary and Anne: "I am asking you if you will be among our party of women?"

"Yes! Of course!" said Mary fervently. "How could you think to stop me from helping Father?"

The countess turned to Anne.

"And you, Anne? You are not our family, but we feel you have become part of our family in the time we have known you. Rest assured, we will not think any the less of you if you decide not to help us. This is not your battle. If you decide not to help us, all I ask is that you say nothing about our plan."

"Yes, I'll help," said Anne, and as she said the words she felt a shock of surprise run through her. She was agreeing to help free a prisoner from the Tower, a condemned traitor. If she was caught, then it was quite likely she – along with the other women – would be arrested and executed. This was not her fight. She did not feel strongly about the battle for the throne between Protestants and Catholics. But she did know that the family had been kind to her, and had treated her fairly. And that Mary loved her father. And that the earl was brave, and a true and honest man. Yes, she would help.

The next day, Anne accompanied Mary, the countess and Louise to the Tower of London to see the Earl. It was the first time Anne had been to the Tower.

Mary had told Anne that when her father had been captured at the Battle of Preston, there was hope he would be released and allowed to return to Dumfriesshire, and be tried in the north, possibly in Carlisle. But when it became obvious that Parliament was determined to make sure there was no such uprising again, and the earl and the other rebels were going to be locked in dungeons in the Tower of London to await trial, the countess moved to London, to be on hand for any support her husband needed. With her she bought her most trusted servants, and then added others from London, all Catholics like Anne.

Anne was shocked when she saw the earl up close. During his trial at the House of Lords he had seemed fit and healthy, standing there firm and upright, his voice strong and booming. Seeing him now, in the confines of the cell, he looked shrunken and haggard. He forced a smile as the countess, Louise, Mary and Anne entered the cell.

"Mary," he said, surprised. He shot an accusing look at his wife. "I told your mother it was best for you not to see me in here."

"I felt I needed to come," said Mary.

The earl sighed.

"Always strong-willed and obstinate," he said. He looked ruefully around the cell. It was a large room, with a barred window high up in one wall, well out of reach. The door was of solid heavy metal, with a barred window in it. Straw was spread on the floor, and there was a bucket in one corner. The stench of urine and faeces from the bucket made Anne realize why the earl had tried to prevent Mary from coming to see him.

Mary went to her father and put her arms around him and squeezed him tightly to her.

"I would rather see you like this than not see you at all, Father," she whispered.

He sighed again.

"These are not the best conditions," he said sadly.

"Have they set a date yet?" asked the countess.

The earl forced a smile.

"Straight to business, my dear?" he asked. "Don't you want to indulge in small talk first?"

The countess went to her husband, put her arms around him and hugged him, and Anne heard her whisper: "There will be other times for small talk. Do they have a date?"

The earl looked at her, surprised, then nodded and said: "The 24th. In two days." He gave a rueful smile. "I believe Parliament are keen to put an end to this situation."

"Two days," nodded the countess thoughtfully. "Very well. We don't have much time."

The earl regarded her, a puzzled expression on his face.

"I don't understand," he said. "Are you hoping for a reprieve for me? I don't think that is likely."

"Who knows what may happen," said the countess. "Now, let us sit down and have our small talk." And she released her husband, and Louise and Anne dragged three chairs to a space away from the stink of the bucket so that the countess and Mary could sit down and talk to the earl in relative comfort.

They chatted, and even laughed as the earl made jokes about being captured at Preston.

How strange, thought Anne. Here we are talking and laughing together like any ordinary family with their servants, yet the earl is sentenced to hang in just two days' time. Finally, it was time for them to leave.

As the door was opened by the guard and Anne walked out of the cell, she made sure she took in details of the area just outside. If she was to be part of this plot, she wanted to play her part well. And she wanted all of them to get away safely afterwards.

She hadn't taken in all the facts about the Tower as they'd come in; she had to admit she'd felt overwhelmed just by being there. But now, as the women retraced their steps to the main gates, every aspect of that formidable castle lodged in Anne's mind.

The cell where the earl was kept was separate from the other cells, on a landing on its own. A stool was placed outside the cell for a guard to sit on, to make sure that no one went in without permission.

A flight of stone steps led down to a corridor that contained other cells. In this corridor, two guards kept watch, taking turns to walk the length of the corridor, listening at the cell doors.

This corridor led to an outer room, and then out onto a courtyard. Across the courtyard was a second building that had to be passed through, before reaching the outer wall of the Tower. Guards were on duty at all the doors of this second building, and the doors were locked. To gain the attention of one of the guards inside the second building, you had to knock at a door. Then a small panel in the door was slid open and the guard looked out and checked to see who was knocking, before unlocking the door.

Another guard was on duty at the exit from this building, unlocking the door to the final outer yard and checking everyone who left.

Finally, there were the main gates of the Tower: huge oak gates with iron straps across them, firmly locked and barred. Two sentries were on duty by this main gate inside a small shelter. As the party approached, Anne's heart gave a leap of panic as she saw the sentry come out from the shelter and look at them, studying the women's faces. If he did the same when they were bringing the earl out, they'd be caught for sure!

The more Anne thought about it, the more impossible the plan seemed.

When they got back to their house, the countess sent messages to the other women who'd agreed to help with the plan. Some were family, others friends.

"We go in tomorrow night," the countess told them. "As soon as it becomes dark. I will arrange our carriages for six o'clock. Make sure you wear long cloaks with hoods, and as many layers as you can beneath."

When the other women had departed, the countess said thoughtfully to Louise, Mary and Anne: "I wonder if we should bring Father McCree along with us. A priest may add to our appearance of innocence."

"No!" blurted out Anne before she could stop herself.

The countess gave Anne a sharp look.

"Why on earth not?" she demanded. "He is our family priest!"

It was Mary who saved Anne. "Because he is … weak," said Mary. "If he knows what we are going to do, his nerve will fail him and he will do or say something that will betray us."

Mary does not trust him, either, thought Anne. For all his words of rebellion, he will betray us if it benefits him.

The countess turned to Louise.

"What do you think, Louise?" she asked.

Louise hesitated, then she nodded; "I agree with Mistress Mary. I think it would be better to arrange for the Father to visit his Lordship on the day set for his execution."

"But we will be gone by then, if all goes well," countered the countess.

Louise bowed slightly.

"Yes, my lady, but the good Father does not need to know that, before the event."

The countess hesitated. It was obvious to her from their manner that Anne, Louise and Mary all distrusted the priest, and that went against everything she believed: that the priest was the voice of God. But, her husband's life was at stake.

"Very well," she said. "We shall keep this just amongst us. I just hope Father McCree doesn't think harshly of us when he discovers we have deceived him."

"Oh, I don't think he will," murmured Anne.

"In fact, I think he will be grateful he didn't know about the plan," added Mary.

"The Countess of Nithsdale to see her husband," announced the countess, as the small hatch in the door of the Inner Tower slid open and the face of the guard looked out at her.

The guard looked past her at the other nine hooded women, of varying heights and shapes.

"Who are they?" the guard demanded.

They had encountered the same question at the main gate.

"Family," answered the countess. Then her voice dropped and she added in a querulous tone: "My husband dies tomorrow. This is our last chance for us all to see him and pray with him for his soul. And, for your indulgence, we bring a token of our gratitude."

The countess held up a small leather bag and shook it so that the chink of coins could be heard; while Louise held up a bottle of brandy.

Immediately the hatch slid shut and the door opened. Coins and the bottle changed hands.

"I am sorry to your family for your grief, milady," grunted the guard, lowering his eyes.

It had been the same scene at the main gate: the money and the bottle of brandy taken, condolences expressed; and the ten hooded women sweeping in.

The same procedure was followed at the door to the main prison building across the courtyard. Then it was along the corridor and up the stairs to the lone cell where the earl was imprisoned. The guard sitting on the stool outside the cell looked startled at the large number of women who appeared to surround him; but the chink of coins being pressed into his hand, and the bottle of brandy allayed his fears. Like the guards before him, he expressed his condolences and sympathy as he unlocked the cell door.

The earl was on his feet, looking stunned, as nine of the women entered his cell. Louise remained outside with the guard to talk to him, tell him of their sorrow at the loss of their dear Lord, and to listen sympathetically to the guard's own tales of woe, of which there would surely be many. Louise's main purpose was to keep him from looking into the cell.

"What's this?" The earl demanded, bewildered as the women gathered around him.

Anne stood back as the countess and Mary hurried to him and hugged him close.

"We're taking you out, Father," said Mary.

"Out?"

"Ssssh!" Mary shot a glance at the cell door, but the guard and Louise must have been in deep and absorbing conversation, because there was no intervention from the direction of the cell door.

Quickly, the countess explained the plan: that the earl was to be dressed in clothes the women would give him, and then they would leave together.

"No!" whispered the earl. "I won't let you risk your lives this way!"

"My life without you is nothing," said the countess firmly.

"But what about the others?" appealed the Earl. And he looked at Anne and the other women, all wearing their hooded cloaks.

"We know what we're doing, and we're doing it willingly," said Anne.

"Now, hurry," said the countess. "There is a carriage waiting."

The earl looked at the faces of the women in front of him, and then finally back at his wife.

"I won't place you in danger," he insisted.

The countess glared at him.

"I thought you were the best man I had ever met, William," she said firmly, but keeping her voice low. "Intelligent, amusing, honest and loyal. Don't show me that I was wrong: that you are stupid and not loyal enough to want to be with me."

"I *do* want to be with you," appealed the earl earnestly.

"Then, if you love me, if you love Mary, respect us and what we want."

The earl studied his wife's face, still looking bewildered and torn, and then he drew her to him and clasped her tight.

"I do love you," he said, his voice filled with passion. "Come, give me the clothes."

The women gathered round the Earl, and then, one by one, hidden from the cell door by the press of women, they removed a layer of clothing from beneath their cloaks, and helped the earl put it on. While this was going on, one of the women watched the cell door to make sure the guard was being kept occupied by Louise. She was relieved to hear the guard talking, telling Louise his life story, as he drank from the brandy bottle, while Louise listened and nodded sympathetically.

Finally, the countess took off her hooded cloak and gave it to her husband, revealing that she wore a second cloak beneath the first.

Anne and Mary went to the bench where the earl had slept during his imprisonment, and stuffed some of her extra clothes beneath the blankets so that it looked as if there was someone asleep on the bench. When they were satisfied that the shape on the bench looked realistic enough, they returned to the rest.

"Now for the test!" whispered back the countess.

The countess went to the cell door and knocked at it. The guard's face appeared in the small barred window.

"We're ready to leave," said the countess, her voice low and sad.

There was the click of the key in the lock, and then the door swung open. The hooded women, with the disguised earl in the middle of them, made their way out of the cell and joined Louise by the stone steps.

"I've given my husband brandy to help him sleep," the countess told the guard. "I would prefer him not to have to think about tomorrow. I would be most grateful if you could ensure he is not disturbed."

And, once again, she opened the leather bag, but this time, instead of taking a few coins, she emptied the remaining coins into her hand and offered them to the guard. He bowed and took them.

"Rest assured, my lady, he won't be disturbed until the morrow," he said. "I give you my word."

The countess nodded and gave him a grateful smile. Then she cast one last look back into the cell, towards the shape on the bench, and blew a kiss. "Till tomorrow, my love," she said.

She nodded to the guard, who shut the cell door, and locked it.

As the group pushed their way down the narrow stone staircase, Mary hissed at her mother in alarm: "You have given away the last of our money. We may yet need some at the other gates!"

The countess gave a grim smile and produced another small leather bag, and shook it, and Mary heard the chink of coins.

"I have a reserve," she announced.

Their journey back through the prison, and across the courtyard and through the next building, went smoothly, helped each time by more coins being produced and tipped into eager palms. As they came out of the last building and looked across at the main gate, Anne's heart almost stopped. There, standing outside the hut by the main gate, was the same guard who had been on duty the previous time they had come to see the earl; the one who had peered into their faces and checked them out so carefully before they left the Tower. He had also been on guard at the main gate when the ten women had entered for this visit, and Anne noticed that he counted the women as they passed through. She had hoped he would have gone off duty when they left; but there he was, waiting for them. He would be sure to count them as they left. The earl would be captured for certain, and all of them arrested as traitors! She had to do something!

Anne stood and let the rest of the women and the earl go past her, their hoods well down over the faces. Once the last had gone, Anne turned and retraced her steps to the inner building, and then crouched down in the dark shadows at the foot of the wall. She hoped that the attention of the guard at the main gate was fully on the approaching group of hooded women, and that he hadn't seen her slide into her hiding place. She crouched low, her knees feeling the wet of the grass through her cloak, and watched as the main gate opened and the hooded figures went through, and she saw that the guard was indeed counting them as they passed him: one, two, three, four, five, six, seven, eight, nine, ten.

As the last went through the gate, the guard pushed the heavy doors shut. Anne counted up to 50, and then she left her hiding place and hurried along the cobbled path to the gate. As she reached it, the guard stared at her in bewilderment.

"Who…?" he began.

"I am sorry," stammered Anne. "I lost my shoe and I had to go back and find it!"

"But who are you? And what are you doing here?"

"I am the maid of Mary Maxwell. We have been visiting her father, the Earl of Nithsdale…"

The guard shook his head firmly.

"All his visitors have already gone," he said.

"But I am still here," pointed out Anne. "So they can't have all gone."

The guard shook his head.

"There were ten who came in, and ten who went out," he said, his voice firm and steady.

Anne shook her head.

"Eleven came in," she said. "The last was the countess's maid. I noticed her arrive late, as you turned away."

The guard stared at her. The firm tone of belief with which Anne stated this had rattled him. Then he shook his head.

"There were ten!" he insisted.

"There were eleven!" replied Anne, equally insistently.

Just then there was a loud banging from the other side of the large main gate. The guard moved to the door set in the gate and opened it, and the countess appeared, hurrying through.

"There you are, Anne!" she said. "We wondered where you had got to! Hurry, the coach is waiting!"

"No!" said the guard, and he stepped to bar Anne's path as she went to move towards her mother.

The countess looked at the guard, bewilderment on her face.

"What do you mean: no?" she demanded.

"I mean that ten women came in through that gate, and eleven are planning to go out."

"There were eleven of us!" insisted Anne loudly.

"If that is the case, let me see them!" snapped the guard.

"Are you calling me and my daughter's maid liars?" demanded the countess, her tone showing her anger.

"If you do not, I will call the Captain of the Guard!" he snapped.

The countess hesitated, then nodded.

"Very well," she said. She turned and called through the gate: "Louise, bring the others through here, if you please. *All* of them."

There was a pause, and then nine hooded figures came through the gate and joined the countess and Anne by the small hut.

"There," said the countess, and she counted them off one by one, finishing with "Eleven. Now are you satisfied?"

"Tell them to take their hoods off," said the guard.

Anne felt as if she was going to be sick. No! she cried out inside. They were all going to be caught, and they had been so near to getting away with the rescue!

"If it will satisfy you," said the countess. She turned to the other nine figures. "Remove your hoods so that this man may see your faces."

One by one, eight of the women threw back their hoods to reveal themselves. Finally, there was just one person left with their hood up.

"Rosa," ordered the countess. "Reveal yourself."

There was a pause, and then the final hood was thrown back to reveal a woman's face. Down one cheek ran a scar.

"You see why Rosa prefers not to show her face," said the countess. "I trust you are satisfied now?"

The guard stared, baffled.

"But...," he began.

"Come, ladies," said the countess. "Our business here is done, until tomorrow."

With that, the ladies pulled their hoods up again and walked back through the door. As they hurried towards the waiting carriages, the bewildered Anne asked the countess: "Milady, how...?"

The countess didn't let her finish.

"Just in case something like that happened, I'd arranged for Rosa to wait in one of the other carriages. When you didn't appear, I guessed we might need her."

"And the Earl?"

"He went off immediately. Mary and I are on our way now to join him at the coast, where a boat waits to take us to France, and sanctuary."

She smiled and patted Anne affectionately on the shoulder.

"A good man's life has been saved today, thanks to your courage."

1716–1790

In 1745 there was another Jacobite rebellion, this one intended to put Prince Charles (Bonnie Prince Charlie), the grandson of James II, on the throne of Britain. As before, this was a Scots-inspired revolt, but it was suppressed with such brutality that it effectively put an end to the Jacobite cause.

At the same time, in London, there was an upsurge in charity, as some of the richer citizens decide they had to help the poorer citizens. Doing good works, and helping others less fortunate, became fashionable. But for many it was more than just a fashion – it was a heartfelt attempt to bring justice to all. At this time, many felt there was no greater injustice than that of slavery.

Slavery had been practised in Britain from before Roman times, with British tribal people being sold as slaves and exported by the Romans. The Anglo-Saxons had also sold local people as slaves.

In the 16th century the slave trade broadened, with English explorers such as Sir John Hawkins buying Africans slaves and transporting them for sale to other countries. By the 18th century the slave trade was a vital part of the British economy: slaves were taken from Africa across the Atlantic to the West Indies and north America and sold to plantation owners who grew crops such as cotton and tobacco. These ships then took the sugar and tobacco, and other goods, from the Americas to England. These same ships then set sail for Africa, carrying trade goods, which they exchanged with local slave traders for more slaves, who were taken to America. This three-way trade (Britain – Africa – America – Britain) became known as Triangular Trade.

By the late 18th century, some wealthy English people had chosen to bring some of the younger slaves – the children – to England to train as household servants.

At the same time, the Abolitionist movement to end the cruel slave trade was starting up. Most of the abolitionists, both in Britain and America, were Quakers (more properly known as The Society of Friends) – a religion that believed (and still believes) in fairness and equality for all, and that humans should work to aid their fellow humans and not coerce them.

Bristol and Liverpool were key ports in this slave trade, but many of the merchants who ran the trade were based in London; London was the main market for selling slave-children as house servants. and it was in London that the Abolition movement began to take shape.

The slave trade 1790

"Michael, your father wants to see you!"

Ten-year-old Michael Baker stopped playing with his toys and looked at his mother, who was standing in the doorway of his room. She was smiling at him, so at least that meant he wasn't in any trouble. At least, he hoped he wasn't. The cook, Mrs Chalmers, had said she'd tell his father he'd dipped his finger in a cherry pie she'd been making. But that had been days ago, when his father was away on business, so he hoped Mrs Chalmers had forgotten about it. Michael's father was often away on business.

"What does he want to see me about?" he asked.

"I'll let him tell you that himself," said his mother. "Now hurry."

As Michael followed his mother to the drawing room, he wondered what was up. His father had been away for almost a week. When he was away on business, he sometimes brought Michael back a small gift. But his father had returned home yesterday evening, and he hadn't given Michael anything yet.

Curious, Michael went into the drawing room. His father was standing by the fireplace, hands behind his back, waiting. He also had a smile on his face, so Michael guessed that this summons was nothing to do with the cherry pie, or anything else he may have done wrong while his father was away.

"Michael," beamed Mr Baker. "You know your mother and I have taken up the cause for the abolition of slavery."

Oh no, thought Michael his heart sinking. *He's going to talk to me about politics.* It was boring enough when his father started talking about religion and everyone's duty to their fellow humans, but when he started talking about politics, Michael had to fight the urge to yawn and fall asleep. Politics was so boring!

"Abolition … yes, Father," said Michael, politely.

"Well, we've decided that spouting fine words isn't enough," said Mr Baker. "The poor people of Africa are treated worse than cattle. But this country grows strong and rich on the back of their badly-used bodies, and their deaths!"

"Yes, Father," nodded Michael. He'd heard all this before, and often.

"Africans are people, the same as you or I," continued his father. "They have the same limbs, the same organs, the same feelings. All that is different is the colour of their skin. Don't you agree?"

"Yes, Father," nodded Michael, wondering how long this speech was going to go on for. Sometimes, when his father got particularly excited about a particular topic he could talk about it for hours; and he often did when his political friends called. Now that he realized he hadn't been summoned to receive a gift, all Michael wanted to do was return to his room so he could play with his toys.

"Good," smiled his father. "Then I think you'll be pleased with the present I've brought you!" To his wife, he said: "Bring them in, my dear."

Michael's heart lifted. There was a gift for him, after all! He wondered what it was? His father had said "them", which meant there was more than one of them, whatever it was. He wondered if it might be some glass marbles? He'd dropped strong hints to his father about how much he enjoyed playing with marbles, and how his friend Edward had a fine collection of them, all different colours. Perhaps his father had brought him back a whole bag of multicoloured marbles, he thought excitedly.

His mother reappeared. Following her into the drawing room came two little children. But they weren't ordinary children. They were black, their skin the colour of a shiny stove. They were both dressed in London style: the boy wearing a neat suit, and the girl a dress with bows and ribbons. They were both small and thin. It was hard for Michael to guess how old they were: he guessed they were a couple of years younger than him. He wondered what they were doing here. Were they carrying the presents his father had brought for him? He looked at them, but neither of the two children appeared to have anything in their hands. The children smiled back at him, shyly.

"Izzy and Mezzo," said his father.

"They're brother and sister," added his mother.

"And now they are *your* brother and sister," proclaimed his father proudly.

Michael felt as if the floor beneath him was wobbling. He felt dizzy. *My* brother and sister? What was his father talking about?

"I bought them yesterday, so that I could give them their freedom," said his father.

"And more than just their freedom," added his mother. "Your father and I are adopting them and giving them our name."

"From now on they are Izzy Baker and Mezzo Baker", said Mr Baker.

No! thought Michael, horrified. This can't be happening! *I* am your son. Your *only* child.

"Well, Michael?" prompted his father. "Aren't you going to say hello to your new brother and sister and make them welcome?"

"Yes. Of course." Michael forced the words out. He also forced himself to smile at the two children. He knew what his father was like, and he didn't want to upset him and make him angry. "My apologies," he said to the two children. "Welcome to our home, and to our family."

"Which is now also your home," beamed Mr Baker at the two children.

"Right now we'd better take them and show them their room," said Mrs Baker. "We have said they can stay together at first, because they might be frightened. They're not used to living in such a house as this."

"Where are they from?" asked Michael, doing his best to seem interested, though inside his senses were shouting: *Take them away! Take them away!*

"They went from Africa on a slave ship to Jamaica," said his father. "But their parents died on the journey, and so a trader decided to make some money out of them by selling them on to be trained as house servants." He gave a rueful smile. "They aren't old enough or strong enough to work the fields yet, otherwise that's where they'd be now. Luckily, there is more money to be made from selling them as house servants in England than there is in Jamaica, which is why they ended up here. They were sent yesterday from Bristol for sale in London because the trader thought they might fetch a higher price here." He shook his head sadly. "It is a cruel trade where human beings are valued like meat." He scowled. "Less than meat. Animals meant for slaughter have a better life than these poor wretches. Did you know that if the captain of a slave ship is running low on drinking water, he will just throw some of the slaves overboard in chains and let them drown. Either that, or let them die in the hulk!"

"I don't think there's any need to persuade Michael of the evils of slavery, dear," said Mrs Baker gently, calming her husband down before he went into a political rant.

"No no, quite right," nodded Mr Baker. "Anyway, Michael, when you are a grown man and look back on this day I know you will feel it to be one of the happiest of your life. But right now, as your mother says, we need to get Izzy and Mezzo settled into the house. Once they are, I hope they will join you in your room and you can share your toys with them."

"Of course, Father," nodded Michael politely. "I look forward to it."

Michael left the room, amazed that neither his father nor his mother had spotted the rage that was coming off him. Two black children from Africa! Slaves! If they'd just been brought in as servants, that would have been fine, but to call them his brother and sister…! He went back to his room, and already he was running through ideas in his head to get rid of them. *I'll take something of Mother's and put it in their room*, he thought. *Then they'll be caught for stealing. Or I'll tell Mrs Chalmers that they made a mess of her cooking and threw it on the floor. One way or another, I am going to get rid of them!*

"He doesn't like us," said Mezzo.

"Mr Baker?" asked Izzy, puzzled. "But he seems so kind! He bought us and freed us…"

Mezzo shook his head.

"The boy, Michael," he said. "He hates us. I saw it in his eyes."

Izzy looked troubled.

"Do you think he'll hurt us?" she asked.

She remembered the beatings they'd suffered on the ship, and later at the port in Jamaica, and then when they'd been loaded onto the dock at Bristol. Treated worse than animals, Mr Baker had said. Yes, thought Izzy, but they were the lucky ones. She'd seen so many others die. Some on the ship from Africa, some killed, some of disease. She was seven years old and in her short life she'd seen far worse things than many people ever saw in their whole lives. But now, she and Mezzo were safe. The kind man and his wife had brought them into their home. And what a home! Izzy had never known such luxury. A real bed, with soft pillows and blankets. The clothes they'd been given were strange to them both, though. As were the shoes. Izzy and Mezzo had grown up wearing next to nothing, just rags tied around their waists, and barefoot. The clothes they'd been given felt tight around their necks, and the boots felt heavy and difficult to walk in. But they'd get used to them – Mr Baker and his wife had given them these clothes, and they wanted to please the couple.

Mezzo thought about her question.

"Yes," he nodded, "he'll hurt us. But not directly. He knows his parents don't like violence. If he beats us, he'll get in trouble, so he'll find another way to hurt us."

"What's he going to do?" asked Izzy.

Mezzo sighed and shook his head sadly.

"I don't know," he admitted. "Before, if people wanted to beat us, they just did it, and no one thought it was wrong. But here…" He looked at the room they were in, their very own proper and comfortable room, and shook his head. "Here, I don't know what'll happen to us. But Michael will make sure it's bad."

Michael went into the kitchen where Mrs Chalmers was peeling potatoes.

"There you are, Michael," she greeted him. "What's the matter? You look like something very bad's happened."

"Have you seen those two children Pa brought home?" Michael asked warily, not sure if Mrs Chalmers was going to be on his side or not.

"I have indeed!" smiled Mrs Chalmers. "And I must say, they looked very pretty, all done up in those clothes. They'll make the neighbours sit up and look, that's for sure." She chuckled. "Mrs Witts will be so jealous. They bring a touch of the exotic to a house. There's a man in Dunby Street who's got a black butler, and everyone is jealous of him because of it. But we've got *two* of them!"

"Father and Mother say they're adopting them," said Michael. "That they're going to be my brother and sister."

Mrs Chalmers shook her head.

"He means they're your brother and sister in the eyes of God, like all human beings," she said. "You know what your father's like about his religion."

"No," Michael corrected her firmly. "He says he and Mother are really going to adopt them. They're going to have our name as well. Baker."

Mrs Chalmers looked at him, puzzled.

"I thought he bought them as servants," she said. "I thought they were to help me around the house."

Michael snorted.

"That's not what he told me," he said. "My brother and sister, he said. They'll be called Baker." He looked slyly at Mrs Chalmers. "They'll be able to tell *you* what to do, and order you about."

Mrs Chalmers laughed. "They can try," she said. "No one orders me about. Not even your mother and father. When they try to, I remind them what your father's always saying about us all being created equal." She laughed again, and carried on peeling the potatoes.

Michael went back to his room and sat on the floor among his toys. He supposed he'd be expected to let that pair of slaves play with them. Well, he wouldn't, he decided fiercely. He'd destroy them before *that* happened. He looked at his toys and wondered which ones he'd get rid of first. The ones that would burn easiest. He'd sneak them down to the kitchen when Mrs Chalmers wasn't there, and put them in the oven of the kitchen range. The others he'd break up and throw away. It was bad enough he had to share his parents with those two, but he wouldn't share his toys, that was for sure!

He heard the sound of the door handle being turned, and he looked up to see his mother smiling at him. Behind her, he could see *them*. He couldn't even bring himself to say their names, he hated them so much.

"I've shown Izzy and Mezzo their room, and where things are in the house," said Mrs Baker. "I think it would be nice if you took them for a walk and showed them the neighbourhood."

Never! thought Michael. The thought of walking along the street with these two, as if they were his *equals*...! Then an idea hit him. They were only young, younger than him. He could take them out into the street, and get them lost. The streets in this part of London could be very confusing, especially for strangers. He'd lead them into one of the more dangerous areas, where crooks and thieves lived, and then sneak away from them. The two would make a perfect target, especially with their fine clothes. Then he'd come home and pretend to be upset and tell his mother and father that they'd got lost, and that he'd spent a long time looking for them but there was no sign – they must have run away. After all, they were just slaves, and the chance of running off and selling the fine clothes they'd been given must have been too good to miss.

"Of course I will, Mama," he said. "That's a good idea."

Michael wasn't sure how long they'd been out. It must have been at least an hour, he thought. At first Michael had taken Izzy and Mezzo along the streets immediately near to their own road. The whole time the people they'd passed had gawped at them. Most of them had never seen a black person before. Michael did his best to ignore the onlookers. In fact, he did his best to ignore Mezzo and Izzy. For one thing, he wasn't even sure if they'd understand him. He wasn't sure what language they spoke. Every now and then they put their heads together and whispered to one another in low tones, and Michael tried to overhear them, but if they were speaking English, their accents were too strong for him to understand them.

Michael had carried on walking, gradually moving further and further away from the house, twisting and turning down alleys and side streets. He wanted to make sure that when he gave them the slip, they wouldn't find their way back to the house. But he knew he'd have a hard time getting away from them. They stuck closely to him as he walked, gazing up at the buildings they passed.

I bet they've never seen anything like London, thought Michael. *All they've ever known is the jungle, the slave ship, and the plantation. They'll be helpless when I finally get rid of them. Helpless and confused.*

He set off down a side alley, and suddenly stopped as he realized where he was. It was a narrow cobbled rat-run with taverns and inns crammed against one another. He'd passed near this alley once with his father, and his father had hurried on and told him to avoid this place; that it was dangerous.

"Cut-throats and thieves lurk there," his father had warned him. "The sort of people who'd slit your throat for a handkerchief."

So what would they do to Izzy and Mezzo, wondered Michael, dressed as finely as they were?

"Well well," chuckled a deep voice behind him. "What have we here? Lost your way?"

Michael stopped and turned, and saw a man had come out of one of the taverns. He had a livid scar down one side of his face, and a black eyepatch over one eye. As Michael watched, other men came out of the tavern to join him.

"Rich-looking coves, ain't they?" murmured one of the other men. "Look at the outfits they're wearing. They must have cost a pretty penny."

"Even the black ones," said another man. He laughed. "You don't often see them wearing clothes like that, do you?"

Suddenly Michael felt very nervous. The men had gathered in a circle around them. This wasn't supposed to happen, thought Michael. Not to me.

One of the men produced a knife, with a long blade that looked as if it was crusted with blood and tobacco.

"I reckon they'll be a lot happier without those clothes," he said. "What d'you reckon, boys?"

"Yeah," nodded another, and others grunted.

The man pointed the knife blade at Michael.

"But what are we gonna do about this one?" he asked. "The other two may be easy pickings, but this one will talk."

"No I won't!" blurted out Michael. "I won't say a word!"

He wished he hadn't done this. He should never have come here. He could feel himself sweating with fear, but his mouth had gone dry.

"He looks like a rich kid to me," said the man who'd first spoken. "I bet his folks have got money."

"Yes they have!" shouted Michael. "My father's a very important man, and if you do anything to me he'll make sure you're hanged!"

The men looked at Michael, and then at one another, and began to laugh.

"My father's a very important man!" mimicked the one holding the knife. Then he stopped laughing and leant into Michael, who smelled the stale beer on his breath as he snarled: "Then I'd better kill you to make sure you don't say anything."

With that, he thrust the knife towards Michael. Before the blade could connect, Mezzo had grabbed Michael and pulled him sharply backwards, so that the blade slashed at thin air. Then, with a fierce cry, Izzy leapt at the man with the knife and sank her teeth into his wrist.

The man let out a scream of pain, but before he could retaliate, Mezzo had leapt in, kicking at the other men with his boots, and swinging hard punches. Izzy let go of the man's wrist and rushed to attack the others, clawing and screaming at them. The men hesitated, backing away from her, and then they turned and ran deeper into the alley.

"Quick!" shouted Mezzo. "Run!"

And he grabbed Michael by the jacket and began to drag him along to the opening of the alley at speed. Michael's brain was in a whirl.

"Izzy!" called Mezzo, and then the small figure of Izzy was rushing along with them.

They made it to the end of the alley, and then began to run along the next street, until they came to a wider road, filled with respectable people.

Mezzo pulled Michael to a halt, and Michael stood, head bowed, gasping for breath.

Izzy looked behind them.

"We've made it," she said.

They do talk English, realized Michael.

He stood up straight, his head still swimming, still catching his breath. He looked at Mezzo and Izzy, who were both watching him with concerned looks on their faces.

"You OK?" asked Mezzo.

Michael nodded.

"Yes," he said, recovering. "I'm fine." He looked back in the direction of the dangerous alley. Then he turned to look at Mezzo and Izzy. "You saved my life," he said. "Thank you."

Mezzo nodded and gestured at the clothes he and Izzy were wearing.

"They think we're black gentlefolk because of the way we're dressed; but they're wrong. We've had to be strong and fight to survive this far, both of us," he said. "We're grateful to your father and mother for taking us in. We know you don't like us, but we'll protect you. No one can beat us down, not after what we've gone through." He turned and smiled down at his sister. "Izzy is the strongest person I know."

"She's stronger than me," admitted Michael. "She's certainly a lot more frightening."

Mezzo hesitated, then he said: "Michael, we know you'll never see us as your brother and sister–'

Michael held out his hand to Mezzo.

"No one has ever stood up for me like that before," he said. "No one has put themselves in danger for me. That sounds me to like a brother." And Michael held out his other hand towards Izzy. "And a sister," he added, with a smile.

Izzy looked at Mezzo, and the brother and sister smiled at one another, and then reached out and each took hold of Michael's hand.

"Family," said Izzy.

"Family," nodded Michael.

1790–1823

After a long struggle, in 1807 William Wilberforce's Slave Trade Act abolished the slave trade in the British Empire; but people who had already been sold as slaves weren't free until 1833, when the Slavery Abolition Act was passed.

During the early part of the 19th century, London began to spread. It was no longer confined to the old City, within the Roman walls. The gaps between the smaller villages around London closed, and then vanished, as houses, shops and small factories filled them in. London was becoming Greater London. But for many Londoners, these outlying areas, these suburbs, weren't the real "London". London was that great, teeming, overcrowded area from Whitechapel in the east to Westminster in the west, and north to Oxford Street.

In 1812, a boy was born in Portsmouth who would become London's greatest chronicler: Charles Dickens. As a small boy he had an idyllic childhood in Portsmouth, and then in Kent; but at the age of eleven he moved to London to join the rest of his family, who had moved to the capital a few months before. If Charles hoped his happy boyhood would continue in London, he was very much mistaken…

Young Charles Dickens 1824

"Jim, I've got a job for you!" called my boss, Mr Sims.

That's me he was talking to – Jim Baker, thirteen years old. I work at Warren's Blacking Factory near Hungerford Stairs, by the Thames, and Mr Sims is in charge of making sure us workers fill all the pots of shoe blacking properly.

"Yes, Mr Sims?" I asked.

I hoped he might put me in a different part of the factory, because the air around the bench where I worked was thick with the smell of blacking, but it wasn't to be.

"We've got a new boy starting tomorrow," he said. "I want you to show him the ropes. He'll be a bit slow at first because he hasn't done this kind of thing before." He grinned. "In fact I don't think he's done any kind of work before. But the owner wants him brought in as a favour to the boy's family."

"Is he special, then, this boy?" I asked. "A rich kid?"

Mr Sims shook his head and gave a laugh.

"No, the exact opposite, from what I hear," he chuckled. Then he winked, and said, "But that's between us, eh, Jim? Let's say we don't know anything about this boy. Only that he's coming to work here."

"Right-ho," I said. "What's his name?"

"Dickens," said Mr Sims. "Charles Dickens."

Eight o'clock the next morning, on the dot, there he was, waiting in the entrance to our building. He looked about eleven or twelve years old, and he had good clothes on, like a proper gent, but I could tell he was nervous about being here. He looked very pale and kept looking about and sniffing the air, like there was a bad smell in the place. Which there was, of course. Not just the smell of shoe blacking and glue, but also the smell of damp from the river next door, and the rats. Rats always give off a terrible smell, and there were loads of them in our building. They ran up and down the stairs all the time.

"Mornin'!" I greeted him. "You must be Charlie Dickens."

"Charles," he corrected me, in a cold voice. He sounded like he'd had a good education.

So, a stuck-up toff, I thought. *Right, we'll soon knock that out of you.* Still, I wasn't going to let him see he'd got to me. After all, for all his good clothes and his posh voice, he was going to be working in the blacking factory, stuffing boot polish in pots, the same as the rest of us.

"My name's Jim Baker," I said. "I've been told to show you the ropes. You ever worked in a blacking factory before?"

He glared at me as if I'd just insulted him, but I also noticed that his lower lip trembled, like he was doing his best to stop himself from crying. I guessed he was really out of his depth here.

"No," he said.

"Don't worry, you'll soon get the hang of it," I said. "How old are you, Charles?"

"I'm twelve years old," he said. Then he added, awkwardly: "My twelfth birthday was two days ago."

Not much of a birthday present, to be sent to work in a blacking factory in this place, I thought. Especially for a toff like this boy, all dressed up and talking posh. I wondered why it had come about? Then I remembered what Mr Sims had said to me, when I'd asked if he was a rich kid. "No, the exact opposite, from what I hear."

So it was money, then. I wondered what had gone wrong for him. Had his family fallen on hard times? Was that why this posh kid was being sent out to work? Maybe his family had died and he'd become an orphan, and that was why he had to go out to work.

Still, none of that was my business. My job was to show him the ropes.

"Right, well, the boss has given you a nice place to work, out of the way of the rest, so to speak. Follow me."

And I led him to a table and chair in a nook under the stairs. There were loads of earthenware pots, like small flower pots, each one filled to the brim with black boot polish, already on the table, with more pots stacked on the floor. Near them were sheets of oiled paper, sheets of blue paper, and string. Also on the table were piles of labels advertising "Warren's Best Shoe Polish", a pot of paste and a brush, and a pair of scissors.

"This is what you do," I said, and I set to work explaining the work to Charles, doing it myself so he could see how it was done.

"First, you put a sheet of the oiled paper on the top of the pot, then pull it down over the rim. That stops the polish leaking out if the pot goes on its side. When you've done that, you put the blue paper over the oiled paper, and pull that right down. Then you tie them both to the rim with the string." I pointed at a groove in the pot, just below the top. "Put the string in there an' tie it tight so it won't pop out. When you've done that you trim it nicely, as close as you can with those scissors. Then, when you've put lids on a gross of 'em, you paste one of those labels on each pot. You know what a gross is, do you?"

"Of course," said Charles. "A gross is a hundred and forty-four."

"Good," I said. "So, that's all there is to it. Have you been told what your hours are?"

Charles shook his head.

"I was just told to be here by eight o'clock this morning," he replied.

"The hours are eight o'clock in the morning till six in the evening. That's ten hours a day, six days a week. We get one day off, on Sundays. You get a break at twelve o'clock for lunch, and a tea break in the middle of the afternoon. Did you bring anything to eat?"

"Yes," nodded Charles. He produced a paper bag from his pocket. "I bought a pie and a piece of cheese."

"Well if you want my advice, keep 'em in your pocket," I told him. "Some of the rats in here are as big as cats, and they'll grab 'em and run off with 'em if they get the chance."

As I spoke, a huge rat appeared from between the floorboards, jumped on the table where the pots were, and then ran up the stairs. Charles stared after it, looking even paler.

"See?" I said. "Have you got a stick?"

"A stick?" asked Charles.

"Yeah. Just in case they get a bit too close. Usually, if that happens, all you have to do is wave a stick at them like you're going to hit them and they'll run away."

"No," said Charles. "I don't have a stick."

I looked around, and saw a broken piece of banister lying on the floor, and gave it to him.

"Here you are," I said. "There's usually bit of old wood lying around. Most of it's rotten, on account of how damp it is. That's 'cause we're right next to the Thames. Anyway, you wave that piece of banister at them, the rats'll soon scarper."

With that, I left him to it and went to my own bench in the main body of the factory, a big room where there were about ten of us boys all putting labels on pots of shoe blacking, the same as Charles was doing. Once Charles had been here a while and had got the hang of it, he'd join us in the big room. All the new boys were put in that same spot under the stairs when they first started. It was to make sure they concentrated and learned how to do the job properly. In the big room, although we all worked hard, we all chatted as we did it. That was okay once you knew what you were doing, but too much nattering to others while you were still learning could lead to slip-ups: tops or labels not stuck on properly, or – even worse – a pot knocked over and the blacking spilled out of it.

"What's the new kid like?" asked my pal Bob Fagin, as I took my place at the bench next to him.

"Posh," I said. "He talks stuck-up, and by the look of his nice hands I don't think he's ever done any sort of hard work before. But he seems all right."

Bob chuckled.

"This work'll test him," he said. "Let's see if he can stick it."

"I bet he don't," piped up Pip Huggins. "I bet you he packs up and goes before dinner time."

"How much d'you bet?" Bob challenged him.

Pip hesitated. Then he said: "Sportsman's bet."

We all laughed. Pip was known never to put his hand in his pocket if he could avoid it, whereas Bob was always ready to put a farthing on anything for a bet.

"Sportsman's bet it is!" grinned Bob.

At twelve o'clock I went along to the nook under the stairs, and found Charles still there. So, Pip had lost the bet.

"Dinner time, Charlie ... Charles," I said.

Charles looked up at me, miserably. His hands were stained deep black from the boot polish, and the pots he'd labelled were stacked up at one side on the floor.

"Is there anywhere I can wash my hands so I can eat my food?" he asked.

"Wash your hands?" I chuckled. "Charles, the water here is filthier than your hands are."

He looked as if he was about to burst into tears.

"But how can I eat?" he begged.

"Just wipe your fingers on your trousers," I told him. "That's what we all do."

Charles looked down at his nice clothes, horrified.

"I can't!" he whispered.

I sighed.

"Okay," I said. "I'll go and find you a rag or something."

I had to admit, I felt sorry for him. For all his lah-di-dah way of speaking and his good clothes, he'd stuck to the work. Four hours of sticking tops and labels on pots of blacking ain't easy when you ain't used to it.

When I got back to the main room, the first words Bob and Pip asked were: "Is he still here?"

"Yes," I nodded.

"Yes," roared Bob in delight. "I win!"

"Sportsman's bet!" Pip reminded him hastily.

I picked up a rag and headed back.

"Where you off to, Jim?" asked Bob.

"I thought I'd keep the new boy company for a bit," I said.

It was a tradition that we left the new boy on his own at his table under the stairs on the first day. After that, we invited him to join us in the main room for dinner time. In a way, it was a kind of test, seeing if he could last. But I felt sorry for Charles. He wasn't tough like the rest of us; but I admired the way he'd lasted the morning, and I wanted to give him a bit of a helping hand. After all, that's what Mr Sims had told me to do. Show him the ropes. Settle him in.

I went back to Charles's table and handed him the rag. He wiped as much of the blacking off his fingers as he could while I took a pie out of my pocket and bit into it.

"So, do you live local, Charles?" I asked.

"Gower Street, Camden Town," he said.

I knew it. Nice, big houses; about three miles north from Hungerford Stairs. But not easy travelling at this time of year, February, because it was still dark when we started work. And the road wasn't none too good once you got out of the city itself and near Camden Town.

"Catch a coach this morning, did you?" I asked.

"No," said Charles. "I walked. I like walking," he said, defiantly.

No you don't, I thought, *no one likes walking three miles on muddy roads in the dark in the middle of winter when it's freezing cold and damp.* He'd have had to leave his house at about half past six to get to Hungerford Stairs by eight. Money, I guessed. Or lack of it. For all his airs and graces, the truth was that Charles was poor.

"You don't sound local," I said.

"No," said Charles. "Our family have lived in various places, because my father has an important position with the Navy."

"Oh yes?" I asked. "What position?"

Charles hesitated, then he said: "He was a Paymaster."

He may have been once, but not any more, he ain't, I thought.

"I was born in Portsmouth," said Charles quickly, too quick for me to ask any more questions about his dad. "Then we moved to Southsea, then to Chatham, and then Broadstairs. Lately my father was promoted to Somerset House. That's why we moved to London."

"You got any brothers and sisters?" I asked.

"Yes," said Charles. "Brothers and sisters." He gave a proud smile. "My sister Fanny is studying music at the Royal Academy. She's a very talented pianist."

It was the proud smile that did it. It annoyed me. Here he was, in a rat-filled cellar, and being all smug about how his family were so high and mighty, with his dad working as Paymaster for the Navy, and his sister studying at the Royal Academy, which would be costing a fortune. I wanted to take him down a peg or two.

"And here you are sticking labels on pots of blacking for ten hours a day for six shillings a week," I grinned. "It don't seem fair, do it."

Even as I said it I saw the look on his face, and I could have kicked myself. I'd said them to hurt him, and I had.

"I think I'd like to be alone now, thank you," he said.

"Suit yourself," I shrugged.

I took my pie and headed back to the main room. Just before I got there, I turned and took a look at him. Charles had his head down on his arms on the table, and I suddenly thought, *he's crying*.

I didn't speak to him for the rest of the day, except at tea-break in the afternoon when I showed him where the tea pot was so he could pour himself a cup of tea. As he left the factory at six for his three-mile walk home, I nodded to him, and thought to myself: Well, he won't be back tomorrow.

I was wrong. At eight o'clock the next morning, there he was, coming in and taking his place at the table under the stairs.

"Shall I move him into the main room with the rest of us?" I asked Mr Sims.

Mr Sims shook his head.

"Leave him where he is for the moment," he said. "Until he gets used to the work."

So I did. But because I felt guilty for the things I'd said to him the day before, I brought him into the main room when we stopped for dinner time, and introduced him to the other boys. Being stuck at the table where he was, in that corner under the stairs, was a lonely place to be, and I thought it might cheer him up to be with the others. And it did.

By the end of the week he seemed a bit happier, even though he kept himself very much to himself and didn't say much. That was mainly because if he started to say something it was usually about his sister, Fanny, and her music, or about his family's life in Broadstairs, and when the boys heard him starting to talk in his posh voice about such lah-di-dah things, they jeered at him and made rude comments. Not to be nasty, just to take him down a peg or two; but I could see that it hurt him. As a result, Charles shut up and just listened, but I knew he was taking everything in.

One day, after Charles had been at the factory about two weeks, I noticed that he hadn't joined us for dinner, so I went to his nook to chase him up. He was sitting at his table, and though he wasn't actually crying, I could tell he was very close to it.

"Come on, Charles," I said. "It's dinner time."

He didn't speak, just nodded, and when I saw his lips trembling I realized that he was afraid that if he opened his mouth he might burst into tears. I hauled over a rickety chair and sat down beside him.

"Charles," I said. "I know that something bad has happened. I can tell by your face. Now you don't have to tell me, but – as someone who's had a lot of bad things happen to him – I can tell you it can sometimes make things seem better."

"Not this," whispered Charles, and his words were so choked and faint I could hardly hear them.

"Has someone died?" I asked.

Charles shook his head.

"Someone about to die?"

Again, he shook his head.

"Then trust me, it ain't as bad as you think."

"Yes it is," said Charles. He hesitated, and then he said: "My father's been sent to prison."

And with that he began to cry, but silently, his body shaking with big sobs.

I looked around and was relieved to see that none of the other boys was anywhere near us.

"Sssh!" I urged him. "Why?" I asked.

"B-because of debt!"

I stretched out a hand and put it gently on his shoulder.

"Yeah, all right. Calm down. Take a deep breath. Come on, breathe."

Charles did as I said, andtook a deep breath, and then another.

"Have you got a wipe?" I asked.

Charles nodded, and took a handkerchief from his pocket and wiped his eyes.

"Going to prison for debt ain't a big thing," I told him. "It can happen to anyone. Look at me, I ain't got no money. I live from one week to another on the money I earn here, and I usually run out two days before pay-day." I gestured with my thumb at the main room. "It's the same with my family and with most of the other people who work here. Everyone runs out of money and takes something to the pawnbroker and hopes they'll have the money to redeem it at the end of the week. But most times, we ain't got the money. That's the way life is. It's the same for most people. Even the poshest people owe money! In fact, my uncle says the poshest people are the worst! And he should know, he's a tailor and he's always having to chase them for their bills. He's had to put quite a few into the Marshalsea, I can tell you."

"That's where my father is," said Charles mournfully, and I could have bitten my tongue off. The Marshalsea is the biggest prison for debtors in London, just along the Thames near Southwark.

"What happened?" I asked, still keeping my voice low and hoping my being out here with Charles wouldn't b ring any of the other boys along to find out what was happening.

Charles took another deep breath, and then it all came out. How he and his family lived in a big house with servants, and had everything they wanted.

"But it turns out that all the money we spent was borrowed. My father ran up bills with different tradesmen, and finally one of them insisted he either paid him the forty pounds he owed or he would take my father to court over the debt."

Forty pounds! Why, that was as much as some people earned in a year, if they were lucky!

"What was the bill for?" I asked. "Clothes? Furniture?"

Charles shook his head.

"It was from the baker's."

I stared at him.

"Forty pounds for a baker's bill?"

"My mother and father thought it important to spend money on the very best cakes when entertaining," said Charles gloomily. "They liked to impress people."

I was about to say "I bet they're impressed now!", but I decided it would only make him even more unhappy, so instead I said: "Still, they allow families to live with the prisoners at the Marshalsea, so if you all move in with your dad you won't have as far to come to work."

At that, his face fell even further.

"That's the worst part of it," he said, and I thought he was going to cry again, but he stopped himself. "My family have moved in with him. All except me."

I stared at him, shocked.

"What?"

He nodded, his face a picture of misery. "My mother, my brothers and my youngest sister have all gone to stay with him there, but my mother says that…" He faltered and his head sunk down. Then he took a deep breath again, lifted his head and told me: "She says that as I am the earner of the family they cannot risk me being associated with that place by having it as my address. So she's made arrangements for me to lodge with a friend of hers in College Street. She says Mrs Roylance will not charge me much in the way of rent, so I will still be able to give her and my father a reasonable sum from my wages so they can pay their daily expenses at the Marshalsea. And they also want me to put money aside from my wages to repay my father's debt."

I stared at him, shocked. No wonder he was so upset. It was bad enough to have the shame of his father in Marshalsea, but for the rest of the family to go in there as well and deliberately leave Charles on his own, and in a strange lodging house at just twelve years of age, so he could work ten hours a day in this place to earn money to keep them in comfort was one of the cruellest things I'd heard. And as for paying off his father's debt of forty pounds! I did a quick calculation. Charles earned six shillings a week. By the time he paid his rent, gave his parents money towards their costs in the Marshalsea, and bought his own food, he'd be lucky if he had a shilling left over. With twenty shillings in a pound, it would take Charles 800 weeks to pay off his father's debt of forty pounds. That was more than fifteen years!

Charles's head had sunk down again.

"I am so miserable!" he moaned. "I'm going to be stuck in this place for ever! Ten hours a day, my skin getting dirtier and dirtier from boot polish! I shall have to wear these same clothes until they turn to rags! I am the poorest and most miserable and unhappiest child in London!"

And this time his head did sink down onto his arms on the table.

For a minute, I didn't know what to say. I tried to think of something to cheer him up, but when I thought about his situation, there wasn't a lot I could say that would make him feel better. And then I had a thought.

"I bet you're not," I challenged him.

He looked up at me, defiance in his face.

"If you're going to say about the people in prisons waiting to be executed, or dying in a workhouse…"

"No," I shook my head. "I'm talking about children, the same age as you and me. Even younger. Not in prison. Not in the workhouse. I bet you I can find one in this same road where we are, who's a lot worse off than you."

Charles studied me.

"Who?" he asked. "Where?"

"I'll show you tonight when we finish work," I said. "Is it a bet?"

"I can't afford to bet," groaned Charles.

"Sportsman's bet," I said. "If you agree I'm right, you take back what you said about being the unhappiest child in London."

"I won't," said Charles. "No one can be as miserable as I am."

"We'll see," I said.

That evening at six o'clock, after I'd finished work and tidied my bench, I stood and waited for Charles to tidy his table, and then we went out into the street and walked up the hill.

"Where are we going?" asked Charles.

"The Strand," I said.

Charles gave a hollow laugh.

"Now I know this is a trick of some sort," he said. "Any child who can afford to live in the Strand is a lot happier than I can ever be."

I knew what he was thinking: the Strand was one of the most famous streets in London, a wide road with shops along both sides, filled with luxury goods and wonderful window displays.

"Wait and see," I told him.

When we reached the Strand, I pointed out a small, thin boy holding a broom, standing barefoot by the edge of the kerb. His skin was so pale beneath the dirt it looked more like parchment. His hair was matted and his clothes hung off him in rags.

"There he is," I said. "His name's Joe. He's a crossing sweeper. He's eight years old. He sweeps the dung and muck from in front of people so they don't get their shoes and clothes dirty when they're crossing the street. He's out there in all weathers, rain or shine, snow or fog. He sleeps where he can, mostly on the streets. Sometimes he grabs a space on a roof to get away from drunks and muggers, but most times it's a shop doorway. He's been sweeping that crossing for the last two years, ever since he was six. Some days he gets enough to buy a bit of bread, some days he gets nothing at all."

Charles fell silent. As we watched, a man and a woman wearing expensive-looking clothes stopped by the kerb, and Joe hurried over to them, gesturing with his broom. The man nodded, and Joe set to work, sweeping horse manure out of their path as they walked to the other side of the road. When they got to the other side, the man threw a coin towards Joe. I notice he didn't even look at him, just tossed it at him, but Joe was down on his knees at once, searching for it.

"Any bets that was only a farthing he gave him?" I said.

"Doesn't he have any family?" Charles asked.

I shook my head.

"Not as I'd know," I told him. "I heard someone say he was an orphan, and someone else said he was a runaway. The thing is, he's all alone, and all he's got are the clothes he stands up in, which aren't much good, and that broom."

Charles fell silent.

"Well?" I asked. "Do I win?"

Charles hesitated, then he nodded.

"Yes," he said.

"Don't worry, Charles," I said. "Something will turn up that'll get your dad out of the Marshalsea. And even if it don't, you don't have to stay at the blacking factory all your life. You're clever, you've got brains.

You'll be able to do something to lift you out of this."

"Like what?" Charles said bitterly. "I don't have any skills. I don't have a trade."

I shrugged.

"You can read and write," I pointed out. "That's more than most people can. Why don't you try that for a game? Writing? I'm sure you could get a job as a reporter on a paper, or something. Cleaner than working in a blacking factory, anyway."

We stood a short while longer, watching tiny Joe hovering by the edge of the kerb, shivering as he waited for someone else to appear who wanted to cross the road. Then I said: "Well, I'm off home. See you tomorrow, Charles."

Next morning, as I reached the Strand on my way to work, I saw that Joe wasn't in his usual place. Instead, there was a girl of about ten, holding a broom and sweeping the road where Joe usually worked. I waited until she'd returned to the pavement after clearing the way for a well-dressed woman, and asked her: "Where's Joe? The boy who usually does this bit?"

"Him? Oh, he's dead," she said. "He died in the night. My brother found his body in a doorway down that lane." And she pointed towards the lane to Hungerford Stairs. She tapped the broom she was holding. "So I've taken his place." Then she spotted a smart middle-aged man approaching the road, and nipped off to get in front of him.

"Clear the road for you, guv!" she called out, and began sweeping energetically.

Poor Joe, I thought as I walked down the lane to Hungerford Stairs and the blacking factory. Charles was already inside, and today I thought he looked paler than usual.

"Did you hear about Joe?" he asked, and I could hear real anger in his voice.

"Yes," I said. "Dead in a shop doorway."

"I'm going to do it, Jim," said Charles, and there was a fire to his manner that hadn't been there before.

"Do what?" I asked.

"What you suggested. Write about it. Tell people what's going on. The misery that children in this city are suffering." He gestured around at the damp-smelling building where we were standing. "Children working ten hours a days, six days a week in a blacking factory. Boys like Joe, sweeping the streets for a farthing. The girl who's taken his place. Small boys sent up red-hot chimneys to clean them. Children hanged for stealing a loaf of bread because they're hungry!" He fixed me with a steely glare. "I'm going to tell all our stories, Jim. And I'm going to do my best to make things change! Because things shouldn't be like this!"

1824–1868

Charles Dickens went on to become one of England's greatest novelists, writing many books including *Oliver Twist, Bleak House, The Old Curiosity Shop, Great Expectations, David Copperfield* and many more. Most of them feature a child or young person who is treated unjustly and cruelly. In *Little Dorrit*, Little Dorrit's family has been incarcerated in Marshalsea Prison because of her father's debts for so long that she was born there.

Much of Dickens's work prompted an outcry at the appalling social conditions he exposed, especially concerning children, and helped to speed up changes to the laws protecting children's welfare.

From 1831 until 1925, London was the world's largest city. The problem was that building, water supplies and sanitation hadn't kept pace with the increase in population, so in many parts of London overcrowding was normal, with many families crammed into single, small houses. The result of massive overcrowding and the dreadful insanitary conditions was an outbreak of cholera in 1848 that killed 14,000 Londoners. Cholera returned in 1866, this time claiming the lives of 6,000 Londoners.

But a new infrastructure for London was being built.

In 1837, when King William IV died, his niece, Victoria, became queen at the age of just nineteen. Three years later Victoria married her cousin, Prince Albert of Saxe-Coburg and Gotha, who became Prince Consort. His arrival in Britain coincided with the sudden development of new engineering methods, and in 1851 Prince Albert organized a exhibition to inform the public about the new technologies being developed in Britain and in other countries. This was the Great Exhibition of 1851. The exhibition was housed in a brand-new building, specially created for the occasion, called the Crystal Palace, a huge structure made of glass set in a cast-iron frame and erected in Hyde Park.

During Victoria's reign, London really expanded as a city, growing upwards and outwards. Steam engines replaced sails for ships, and more and larger trading ships were built. More docks were built to keep pace with the demand for imports and exports. London expanded eastwards along the Thames as docklands developed.

All these industries and all this new building meant workers were needed, both in the factories and in offices. People flocked to grab the jobs that were created, coming from the north of the country, from Ireland, from Wales, and from Scotland. In 1800 London's population stood at 1 million. By 1881 it had grown to 4.5 million, making London one of the most crowded cities on the whole planet. All of this led to more houses and factories being built, more waterworks being laid, and more railway lines and stations springing up to carry all these people. It was at this time that the great age of railways developed. London at the heart of the system with its major railway termini: Paddington (opened in 1834); Euston (1837); Fenchurch Street (1841); Waterloo (1848); Kings Cross (1852); Victoria (1862); and Charing Cross (1864).

In 1862 work began on what was to become one of the most stunning examples of Victorian railway station engineering: St Pancras station. It featured a huge curved glass roof and a palace-like hotel.

By 1868 St Pancras station was ready. Prince Albert had died in 1861, and many felt the new station would be a fitting memorial to the late prince as he'd embraced and promoted the new advances in technology. His widow, Queen Victoria, was invited open the new station. For the queen, this was an opportunity for her children to become involved in the celebration of their father's life, especially her youngest and favourite child, Princess Beatrice...

Royal duty 1868

Twelve-year-old Sarah Baker stood in the long corridor inside Buckingham Palace, just outside a big imposing dark oak door. Even with the door closed, she could hear the sounds of the conversation from within the room: the firm, slightly booming voice of Queen Victoria and that of Sarah's mistress, eleven-year-old Princess Beatrice, the queen's youngest daughter. The princess was receiving her orders for an official engagement: in three days' time the brand new railway station at St Pancras was to be officially opened by the queen, and the queen wanted Beatrice to attend the opening with her.

Beatrice didn't want to go. Sarah heard the princess say, "But Mama, do I have to?" The queen then launched into a long harangue about duty, and how the nation looked to the queen and her children as examples of good behaviour, and that she wanted – no, she *insisted* – that Beatrice accompany her to the opening of the brand-new railway terminus in Euston Road.

After that, Sarah had heard just a few words spoken by Beatrice, all of them meek and acquiescent.

The conversation inside the room, ceased; and then the door opened and Beatrice came out. Sarah could see from the red flush of her cheeks and the grim set of her mouth that she was angry. She didn't even look at Sarah, she just set off along the corridor, her feet stamping on the thick plush carpet as she went, with Sarah hurrying after her.

Beatrice said nothing as they mounted the stairs. It wasn't until they were back inside Beatrice's own chambers and the door was firmly shut that Beatrice burst out: "I hate it! I hate everything!"

Sarah hurried to the jug and poured a cup of water for the young princess, hoping it might help calm her down.

"Does Her Majesty insist you go to the opening of the railway station?" asked Sarah, making sure not to let Beatrice know she'd overheard the conversation.

"She does!" fumed Beatrice. "But why?" she wailed. "Why me? I'm never going to be queen! All the boys are ahead of me, Bertie, Alfred, Arthur and Leopold, and then there are all my sisters! Why do I have to go to the opening of this silly station? Why doesn't she take one of the boys?"

"Perhaps she's trying to be fair to you girls," suggested Sarah. "Some girls like trains."

"I don't!" snapped Beatrice. "I bet all the others like trains more than me. Alice, Helen, Louise…" She scowled. "And as for duty, and being examples of good behaviour," she added, mimicking her mother's tone, "she ought to talk to Bertie." Bertie was Beatrice's eldest brother, the heir to the throne, the next king of England. "He lives a disgraceful life, running around with those dreadful friends of his! He's a terrible example. Mother should take him with her and keep an eye on him!"

She sank down heavily on a chair, a moody expression on her face, and gave a heartfelt sigh. "I hate being a princess. It's like being in prison. I can't do anything I want. I can't run about and have fun, and I always have to act like a little lady because 'it's my duty' as Mama says." She sighed again. "You don't know how lucky you are, Sarah."

Not as lucky as you, thought Sarah, wryly, as she looked at her mistress. Beatrice lived in the biggest and best house in London, Buckingham Palace. Sarah lived in a small house with her parents and two brothers and three sisters. Beatrice had servants, like Sarah, to look after every part of her life: to help her bathe, to help her dress, to bring her food. Sarah not only had to take care of herself, she also had to look after her younger brother and two younger sisters, and help around the house and with the shopping.

"Sarah!"

For the first time since they'd left the queen's rooms, Sarah heard joy in the princess's voice. Beatrice was smiling, a mischievous look on her face.

"I've had an idea!"

"Yes, Your Highness?" asked Sarah, warily. She'd been one of Beatrice's maids for just over six months, and in that time she'd come to realize that sometimes the young princess had wild idea, just like any other young girl.

"Why don't we sneak out?"

Sarah looked at Beatrice anxiously.

"Sneak out?" she repeated. "Where?"

"Out into the streets, of course! And just for a day, I could be ordinary Beatrice, not a princess! I could feel what it's like to be an ordinary girl!"

"I don't think that's a good idea, Your Highness," said Sarah cautiously. In fact, it was a very *bad* idea. Very bad indeed.

"Why not?" demanded Beatrice.

"You are the heir to the throne…"

"I'm just one of the heirs to the throne," interrupted Beatrice. "There are loads ahead of me. In fact, I'm so far down the list I'm surprised anyone knows about me."

"They do, Your Highness," Sarah assured her. "And you have to stay here for your safety, and only go out when you're properly guarded."

"But that's what I was just saying!" protested Beatrice. "I can't go out and do anything, without having guards around me! I never get to meet anyone!"

"You meet the important people who come to the palace," countered Sarah.

"I don't want to meet only important people. I want to meet ordinary people. People like … the kind of people you meet, Sarah."

Oh no, thought Sarah, her heart sinking. She knew where this was going, and already she was dreading it.

"Your Highness…" she began.

"Hush!" said Beatrice imperiously, acting every inch the princess. "We shall go out together, and you will introduce me to ordinary people." She giggled. "I'll dress up in a cloak, and pretend that I'm a maid, just like you, and that we're out for the day, two ordinary young girls going about our business."

"It's not a good idea, Your Highness," cautioned Sarah. "If we were found out, I'd be dismissed immediately."

"No you wouldn't," said Beatrice. "I would tell Mama that I forced you. I would be responsible."

"I don't think the queen would take that into account," said Sarah nervously.

"Yes she would," insisted Beatrice. Then she smiled. "Anyway, we must make sure we don't get caught."

Two hours later, Sarah and Beatrice were hurrying along Pall Mall, Beatrice wearing Sarah's spare cloak with the hood up over her head so that she wouldn't be recognized as they slipped out through the servant's entrance at the back of the palace. *This is going to go dreadfully wrong*, groaned Sarah inwardly. *Someone will recognize her.* And there were plenty of people who had no love for the royal family. There had already been two assassination attempts on the life of Queen Victoria herself. If those people who hated the royal family saw the princess on the street, unprotected and unguarded, who knows what might happen.

I should have told the guards, Sarah chastised herself. Or the footmen. They would have stopped her. But there had been no chance to tell anyone; once Beatrice had got the idea into her head, she'd followed Sarah around, trying on her spare set of street clothes, and talking delightedly about what fun they were going to have. *It's as if she doesn't want to let me out of her sight in case I tell someone about her plan*, thought Sarah. Beatrice could be very determined when she wanted something.

"Where will you take me?" demanded Beatrice excitedly.

"To Hyde Park?" suggested Sarah.

Beatrice shook her head dismissively.

"I go to the park all the time," she said. "I ride with Mama there in her coach." A mischievous glint came into her eye. "I want to go to the bad parts of town."

Sarah shook her head.

"I don't think that's a very good idea, Your Highness," she cautioned.

"Yes it is," countered Beatrice firmly. "You say I am the heir to the throne. How am I to govern properly if I don't know how my people live?"

Sarah was on the point of reminding the princess that she herself had said there were so many siblings ahead of her in line to the throne that it was highly unlikely that she would ever be queen in her own right. For that to happen, all her brothers and sisters would have to die: Bertie, Alfred, Arthur, Leopold, Victoria, Alice, Helena and Louise. Sarah agreed with Beatrice – that was very, very unlikely. However, she didn't say it. Sarah was only a maid, and a maid who argued with her royal mistress could find herself out of a job. That was something Sarah couldn't afford to have happen.

"Seven Dials," announced Beatrice. "I have overheard the footmen talk about it. They say it is a very wicked place."

"It is," agreed Sarah. "It's also a very dirty place. There's disease there. All sorts of illnesses. It would not be a good thing if you were to catch something and fall seriously ill. Your Highness is very delicate."

"I will not catch anything," Beatrice insisted firmly. "We are very strong in our family. And I will not be going into any of the houses, just walking through the area, looking."

Sarah's heart sank. Seven Dials was a rat-infested slum, a maze of narrow streets where every sort of crook and low-life lived, amongst ordinary honest but poor people who couldn't afford to live anywhere better. The place was called Seven Dials because seven streets met together in a square. Her mother had told her many years ago there had once been a tall stone column in the middle of this square, with a sundial on each side of the column, which was how the place got its name. The column of sundials had gone long ago, but the name lived on. It was the last place she wanted to go herself, let alone take princess Beatrice. But if she refused, then the princess would be angry with her and would demand she be dismissed.

"If Your Highness insists," said Sarah unhappily.

"I do," said Beatrice.

And so the two girls continued along Pall Mall, heading towards Trafalgar Square. As they walked, Beatrice continued to complain about the official visit to formally open St Pancras station.

"Mama says I must go to this new railway station with her because of what it meant to Papa. She says the reason Britain has such engineering marvels is because of Papa, and we must promote that tradition."

Even though Beatrice said this with a note of petulance in her voice, Sarah knew that it was true. And she knew that, in her heart, Beatrice must know it, also. Prince Albert had helped to create the conditions for engineering to develop in modern Britain. But Sarah didn't say any of this out loud – she didn't want Beatrice to fly into a temper. Instead, she concentrated on where they were going.

At Trafalgar Square, Sarah steered Beatrice towards St Martin's Lane.

"We'll follow this lane, Your Highness," she said. "But I would advise you to keep your head down and move as swiftly as you can. That way it will look as if you know these parts and you won't be troubled. But if you stop and look around, they will know you for a stranger."

"And what will happen to me then?" asked Beatrice, with a smile.

"Beggars will bother you for money," said Sarah. "Perhaps worse. Some will try and rob you. And, if you resist, they can be violent."

Beatrice hesitated. Now she was actually at the entrance to the infamous rookeries, the maze of alleyways, with the smells of excrement and urine and stale cooking, Sarah could tell she was having second thoughts. This place was only a short distance from the wealth and safety of Buckingham Palace, but conditions in Seven Dials were a world away from the life of the royal family. But then Beatrice's face took on that same firm defiant look Sarah had seen so often before. Not just on Princess Beatrice, but on her brothers and sisters, too, and even on the queen herself, when she had been told bad news.

"I am not afraid," said Beatrice flatly. "Let us go in."

"Very well, Your Highness," said Sarah.

As the two girls made their way along the narrow lane, Sarah reflected that whoever had come up with the name "rookeries" to describe these places had chosen well. Just like the branches of trees where flocks of rooks gathered close together in their hundreds, here the houses were crammed close together, each room filled with as many people as they could cram in. Alleys and back streets criss-crossed the main roads, which meant that if anyone was being chased by the police, they could disappear into the maze-like streets and vanish. Not that the police came to places like Seven Dials very often – they preferred to stay away from them and avoid trouble.

An overpowering smell came from the drains and the gutters where foul water ran, and from the dry outhouses that served as toilets, which were filled with human waste.

Most of the children they saw were barefoot, as were many of the women. Most of the men wore boots, but even these were mismatched: one of one size, one of another, one more worn than the other. Sarah noticed this because she kept her head down as they walked, determined to avoid eye contact that could lead to a confrontation, or a begging demand.

We're too well dressed, she thought. Sarah always made sure her cloak was clean and fresh-looking when she went to work at the palace. It wouldn't do for one of the princess's maids to be shabbily dressed. But here in Seven Dials, a decent cloak was out of place.

"Look there!" exclaimed Beatrice.

Sarah turned her head to look at the princess, and groaned inwardly.

Far from keeping her head down, as Sarah had suggested was wisest, Beatrice was looking directly across the narrow street. Sarah switched her gaze to what had caught Beatrice's attention. On the other side of the street, a woman was lying on the pavement. People walking along near her either stepped over her, or walked around her.

"Why aren't those people helping her?" demanded Beatrice. "She's ill! She could be dying!"

Or drunk, thought Sarah.

"It's not a good idea…" she began. But she was too late, Beatrice was already hurrying to where the woman lay. Sarah followed her. As they reached the woman, Sarah's nose picked out the smell of cheap spirits.

"She's drunk, Your Highness," Sarah whispered.

"That may be, but we can't just leave her here," said Beatrice. "She'll die." As a group of four roughly-dressed men came towards them along the street, Beatrice called out: "You there!"

No, wished Sarah fervently. *Please, no! Please let them ignore us and go on their way.*

The men stopped, puzzled by the tone and accent of Beatrice's voice.

"Us?" demanded one of the men.

"Yes," said Beatrice. She pointed to the unconscious woman on the pavement. "This woman needs help."

"Well, help her then," shrugged the man, and he chuckled, while his friends laughed out loud. With that the men moved on.

Good, thought Sarah, relieved. Her relief didn't last long.

"Stop!" snapped Beatrice.

Oh God, no! groaned Sarah. *Please be quiet.*

The four men stopped, and looked at the two girls, puzzled.

"Eh?" queried one.

"Come here and take care of this woman," ordered Beatrice.

At the commanding tone, the man who'd spoken scowled.

"Are you giving me orders?" he demanded angrily.

"No!" blurted out Sarah. "She's just upset!"

"She'll be even more upset when she gets the back of my 'and!" growled the man, and he strode forward, his hand raised ready to hit Beatrice.

Sarah stepped forward swiftly, putting herself between Beatrice and the man. The man's three friends had joined them, expressions of amusement on their faces. This was entertainment, and it was free!

"She doesn't mean anything," pleaded Sarah.

"Yes I do," insisted Beatrice firmly. She pointed again at the woman lying on the floor. "This woman is in need of help. It'll take strong men to carry her to where she lives."

The man hesitated, then he shook his head.

"I don't know her," he said. "She's nothin' to do with me."

"But she's a human being!" insisted Beatrice. "It is your duty as one human being to another to help her!"

The man's eyes narrowed, and now Sarah could see that he was seriously angry.

"No," he grated. "My duty is to shut your mouth up!"

And this time when he pulled his arm back, Sarah was horrified to see his fist was bunched, ready for a hard punch.

"Please…!" Sarah begged.

"Don't beg them, Sarah," cut in Beatrice. "Any man who would strike a woman is no man at all."

The man gaped, shocked.

"What did you say?" he demanded.

"I will repeat it, if you wish," snapped Beatrice. Then she threw back the hood of her cloak and glared at the men. "And take this as a warning. I am Princess Beatrice Mary Victoria Feodore of Saxe-Coburg and Gotha, your future queen. And if you dare to touch me or my maid, I shall see that you are hanged!"

The man stared at her, stunned, his fist still pulled back ready to strike. Then he laughed and turned to his mates.

"Did you hear that, boys?" he laughed. "She's our queen!"

"Future queen," Sarah corrected him in quiet tones.

Then she noticed that the other men weren't laughing. Instead, they all looked uncomfortable. The man with his fist still raised noticed that as well.

"What's up with you lot?" he demanded.

"She might be, Bill," muttered one.

Bill looked at them, bewildered.

"Might be what?" he asked.

One of the other men nodded, then mumbled in awkward tones: "Who she said she is."

The man called Bill looked at them, incredulously.

"You idiots!" he snorted. "What would a princess be doing here?"

"Seeing how my future subjects live," stated Beatrice firmly.

There was a pause while Bill looked at Beatrice, then at Sarah, then at his pals. It was obviously too bewildering for him to take in. One of the men gestured at the woman, still lying unconscious on the pavement.

"Anyway, it can't do any harm to take Peg in," he said. "She could catch her death of cold otherwise."

"Yeah," nodded another. "Sam's right. It's only right, doing the decent thing." He moved to the woman. "You take her feet, Sam, I'll take her head. Joe, you give me a hand as well."

With that, the three men went to the fallen woman and began to lift her up. She muttered as they raised her, but she didn't wake up.

Bill didn't move. He just regarded the two girls suspiciously.

"You ain't really?" he asked, doubt now in his voice.

"I do not lie," said Beatrice flatly. "Now, I suggest that you help your friends. The woman seems heavier than she looks." Then she turned to Sarah. "Sarah, we must go."

And with that, Beatrice headed back down the narrow lane along which they'd come. Sarah hesitated, and turned towards the men, who were still looking stunned.

"I hope Peg's all right," she said.

Then she hurried after Beatrice, and caught her up after a few yards.

"That was terrifying, Your Highness" she burst out.

"Yes, it was," agreed Beatrice, still on the move. Sarah noticed that the princess was breathing hard. She was frightened, realized Sarah, but she refused to show her fear to those men.

"I think it's time we returned to the palace," said Sarah.

Beatrice nodded, and pulled the hood up over her head.

"I think you're right," she agreed.

Two days later, Beatrice and Sarah sat in a horse-drawn coach as it travelled along Euston Road. Ahead of them was another coach, much more ornate in design, in which Queen Victoria sat with her own maids and servants.

Bodyguards and security men rode alongside the coaches on horseback, and on the coaches with the footmen. The roads had been cleared of traffic, and the pavements were lined with people cheering and waving as the coaches passed them.

Sarah peered through the small window at the front of the coach.

"We're approaching St Pancras station, your Highness," she announced.

Beatrice nodded.

"Do you think that Papa would be pleased that I'm here today?" she asked earnestly.

Sarah nodded and smiled.

"I think your papa would have been very proud of you indeed, Your Highness," she said. "And not just because of today." She looked around to make sure she couldn't be overheard, then dropped her voice to a whisper and said: "He would have been especially proud of what you did in Seven Dials."

1869–1940

After Queen Victoria died in 1901, London continued to expand. In 1881 its population was 4.5 million. By 1891 it was almost 6 million, and by 1940 it had grown to almost 9 million.

These were dangerous times for London – and the rest of the world. 1914 saw the First World War, also known as the Great War, between Britain and Germany. Both countries were ruled by Victoria's grandchildren: Germany by Kaiser Wilhelm II, and Britain by George V, so the war could be thought of as a family squabble that ended up engulfing the whole world. Londoners lived under the threat of air raids from Germany's airships, Zeppelins, but luckily for London the air raids actually took place away from the city.

The situation in 1940 was very different. The First World War had been called "the war to end wars", but in 1939, 21 years after the First World War ended in 1918, the Second World War broke out. And this time London was a main target.

Blitz! 1940

BOOOOMMMMMM!!!!

The bomb landed in the next street, but it seemed as if it was right next to me. One minute I was standing with my seven-year-old sister, Annie, holding her hand, and then I heard a whining noise coming down from the sky. I looked up but all I could see were the searchlights in the black sky. The next moment the ground rose up around me, throwing me into the air, and then I was lying on the pavement, dust and smoke all around. Bricks and rubble and bits of metal were flying past, smashing into the pavement and bouncing all over the place. I was aware of a building collapsing, of someone screaming, intense heat as if someone had switched on the biggest gas fire in the world, the sound of rubble raining down, and through it all the heavy drone of the bombers overhead and the bone-penetrating scream of the air-raid siren.

"Annie!" I yelled.

I could hardly see because of all the smoke and dust. I heard crying and reached out to find Annie lying on the pavement.

"I'm scared…" Annie whimpered. "I'm going to die."

"You're not going to die," I told her. I didn't know if it was true, but I felt I had to say something.

I took hold of Annie's arm and tried to pull her to her feet, but all Annie wanted to do was lie on the pavement.

"I'm going to die," Annie moaned again, and then she started to cry great big sobs of fear.

"Get up!" I shouted. "Get up or you *will* die! You've got to get up before another bomb falls!"

That seemed to do the trick. Still crying, Annie stumbled to her feet. I hung on to her arm; I didn't want Annie running off, as I knew I'd never be able to find her in the darkness and smoke. Both of us were covered in thick dust, but in the dark I couldn't tell what colour it was. It looked grey. Was it gas? I was frightened of gas. My grandfather had told me about the gas the Germans used against the British troops in the last war. It got into your lungs from the inside and ate them and you ended up coughing until you drowned in your own blood. I wished Mum was there. And suddenly, she was.

I heard her shout, "Harry!" and then she grabbed hold of me by the collar.

"I told you to get to the shelter!" she yelled angrily.

"We were waiting for you," I said.

"Annie, are you all right?" she asked, bending down and looking into my sister's terrified little face.

"I'm going to die," Annie cried.

"No you're not," said Mum. "Now hold on to Harry's hand and don't let go." To me, she said firmly: "Harry, take hold of my skirt and don't you let go of it whatever happens. And don't let go of Annie's hand."

As I took hold of her skirt in one hand and Annie's hand in the other, Mum turned and called out, "Come on, you! Hurry up!"

For the first time I saw a young woman, standing in the smoke and dust. She was holding a bundle in one of her arms. Then I recognized her as the young woman with the baby who lived in the house next to us. Mum had gone to help her when she saw her trying to carry her baby and her gas mask at the same time – the young woman only had one good arm and couldn't manage them both.

Mum had seen her struggling and had told me: "Go on, Harry. Run to the shelter. Keep hold of Annie. I'll be right along."

But I hadn't run. I'd gone round the corner, and then waited with Annie. I didn't want to go to the shelter without Mum in case she got killed. That was when I'd heard the sound of the bombers overhead. If me and Annie had gone straight to the shelter when the siren had gone off we might have got there before the bombers arrived, but now the the first bomb had been dropped and even in the dark and through the smoke and dust I could see that buildings had disappeared.

Mum grabbed the baby and shouted to me and the young woman, "Right, run!"

We all began to run, Mum holding the baby, me holding her skirt, and Annie hanging on to my hand. Behind us came the young woman. She ran with a funny sort of wobble, and I realized she had a bad leg. I hadn't noticed it before because when I saw her out in the street pushing her pram, she was usually walking slowly, but now she was running I could see that she was wobbling all over the place.

Behind us there was a *BOOM!* as another bomb went off. This one was much further away, but I still felt the ground shake under my feet.

"Keep running!" Mum shouted.

I could feel my lungs hurting and I wondered again if any of the bombs had been a gas bomb. Maybe we should have put our gas masks on, but Mum didn't stop, she kept running.

"Mum!" I yelled. "Gas!"

"There's no gas!" shouted Mum. "Keep running!"

Out of Bayham Street we ran and along Crowndale Road. Past the Post Office, and into Mornington Crescent Tube station.

An air-raid warden was standing outside the entrance to the station wearing his gas mask, and as we got near him he lifted his mask away from his face and shouted angrily: "Where are your gas masks?"

Mum didn't stop to answer him. She ran straight past the air-raid warden, with the baby in her arms and me and Annie close behind her, into the entrance area of the Tube station.

The young woman came stumbling after us, nearly falling over.

Once we were inside the station entrance all four of us bent over, breathing hard, trying to get their breath back. I felt sick with the running. Annie was still crying, great big sobs. Her nose was running. I was still scared that it was gas that made Annie pant and breathe hard, and I wondered if it was the gas that was making her nose run now.

The warden had followed us into the station entrance and he shouted again, even more angry than before: "Where are your gas masks? Why haven't you got them on!"

Mum stood panting for a second, then she held up her gas mask in its brown cardboard box and held it out in his face.

"Here it is," she said, still out of breath. "And if we'd stopped to put them on we'd have been killed by that bomb back there. Satisfied?"

The warden obviously wasn't satisfied, because he got very puffed-up and angry looking.

"What's your name and address?" he demanded. "I shall report you for not using your gas mask properly."

"Oh shut up," snapped Mum. Turning to me and Annie, she said, "Come on, let's get down to the platform."

The young woman came over to Mum and started crying.

"I'm so sorry," she said. "You and your kids nearly got killed 'cause you waited for me."

Mum shook her head.

"No, we nearly got killed because some German dropped a bomb on us."

Mum held out the baby in her arms to the young woman.

"Here," she said. "Get down to the platform and find yourself a space."

The young woman took her baby and went down the stairs to the platform.

The warden obviously wasn't happy. "I'm still going to report you," he said. Then, pointing to me and Annie he said: "And those kids shouldn't be here. They should have been evacuated. You're putting them at risk by keeping them in London with this bombing going on."

"Why don't you mind your own business," said Mum.

"It is my business," said the warden, and he tapped the band he wore round his arm that said "ARP warden".

I was angry with the warden for having a go at Mum after all she'd done, saving the woman and her baby and getting me and Annie safely to the shelter. So I told him: "We were evacuated. Only we came back."

"Then you're more stupid than you look," said the warden.

"It was our dad," said Annie in a small voice. "We came back because of our dad."

The warden looked puzzled.

"What do you mean?" he asked. Turning to me he asked: "What does she mean?"

"She doesn't mean anything," said Mum, very tight-lipped and firm. "Can we go down to the platform, or are you gonna call a copper and have us arrested?"

The warden got very puffed-up and angry again.

"This war isn't a joke, you know. If I see you without your gas masks again, I shall report you. Don't think I won't."

With that the warden put his gas mask back on and went back to the entrance of the Tube station. He looked up to the sky where the moving searchlights criss-crossed as they tried to pick out the bombers.

Mum headed towards the stairs. I took Annie's hand and we followed her, hanging on to the rail that curved round the wall. I didn't want to trip and fall – it was a long way down to the bottom of the steps. We'd hardly gone down a few stairs, when Mum stopped and leant against the wall, her hand to her face.

"Mum?" I asked. "Are you all right?"

Then I realized she was crying.

"Mum?" I asked, bewildered. "What's the matter? Are you hurt?"

A shock of fear went through me as I thought that maybe some shrapnel or something from the bomb blast had hit Mum and she'd been hiding it all this time.

"Mum," I said, even more urgently, "do you want a doctor?"

Mum didn't speak at first, just cried, her head turned away from me. her hand covering her face, her body shaking with sobs. Then finally she took her hand away from her face, shook her head and said, "No," in a small, strangled voice.

She sank down onto the stairs and grabbed me and Annie and pulled us closely to her and hugged us both tightly.

"He's right," she sobbed.

"Who?" I asked, baffled.

"That stupid air-raid warden," she said. "It could have been gas. I should have made you put your masks on, but no one can run when they're wearing those stupid things and you wouldn't have been able to see where you were going… And if I hadn't been so stupid and stopped and looked after that woman and her stupid baby…" And Mum started crying again, letting go of us and dropping her head into her hands. "You both could have been killed because of me."

"No, Mum!" I told her. "You saved us. You saved that woman and her baby. And we couldn't have run wearing the gas masks."

I knew Mum was right about that. The gas masks were terrible to wear, smelling all rubbery with a tiny plastic window that you were supposed to see through but which misted up so you couldn't see anything. They were all right if you were standing still, but you couldn't run while wearing a gas mask. It was like wearing a blindfold, you'd just crash into something or fall over.

Annie was looking very frightened because Mum was crying. Mum hardly ever cried. The only time I could remember her crying was when me and Annie had gone away the year before when the war started, and we'd been evacuated with all the other kids to the countryside. And then when we came back to London again, after Dad went missing.

Mum took a handkerchief from her pocket and blew her nose loudly. Then she wiped her eyes. The hankie left a smear in the black-and-grey dust on her face, showing her pale skin underneath.

"We're going to be all right, Mum," I said. "Don't worry."

My name's Harry Baker. I'm eleven years old and I live with my mum and dad and my little sister Annie in Camden Town, London, not far from the big railway stations at Euston, King's Cross and St Pancras. Mum says that's why the Germans keep bombing our area so heavily, because they want to knock out these big railway stations and stop the trains running.

I still think of my dad as being with us, even though he isn't. When war broke out last year, he joined up in the army and went to France to fight. At the same time me and Annie were evacuated to the country.

Nearly all the kids from the big cities, like London, were sent away to the countryside because the Government expected the Germans to start bombing the cities straight away; but it didn't happen. At least not then.

The couple me and Annie were sent to stay with were a nice old pair called Mr and Mrs Pegg in Northampton. They were very kind to us, which wasn't the case for all the kids who went away. We missed Mum, of course, and worried about her being in London on her own, even though she had our relatives and friends and neighbours close by. And then, in June just gone, I got a letter from Mum telling me that Dad was missing. His regiment had got caught up in the big retreat from Dunkirk, where the British army had been trapped by the Germans. Loads of boats went across the Channel to get the soldiers off the beaches at Dunkirk. They reckon those boats took about half a million soldiers off the beaches and brought them back to England; but Dad wasn't one of them. The letter Mum got from the army said they regretted to inform her that Private Ted Baker was "missing in action".

I couldn't stand the thought of Mum at home alone, even with friends and relatives around her, not knowing whether Dad was alive or dead. So I talked to Mr and Mrs Pegg, and they agreed we could go back to London to be with Mum. After all, there hadn't been any serious bombing raids on London. At least, not in the area we lived in.

When we first got back home, Mum told me off and said we should have stayed in Northampton where we'd be safe, but I could tell she was secretly pleased we'd come back. She was really upset about Dad, and spent a lot of time looking at his photo in the frame on the sideboard, talking to it when she thought I wasn't around to hear her.

It was after me and Annie came back, in August, that the Germans launched their big air attacks, but our fighter pilots mostly managed to keep the bombers away from their targets, which were our airfields. This was called the Battle of Britain, and it ended in September, and we all thought we'd won. But then the Germans launched what they called the Blitzkrieg – or the Blitz, as we called it – which was heavy bombers coming over at night and dropping bombs on what they thought were key targets – like the docks and the big railway stations near where we lived.

When the bombers came over, the air-raid sirens went off and we rushed to the nearest bomb shelter, which was the Tube station at Mornington Crescent. We'd been doing this every night for the last two weeks now. It had been going on for so long that some people were now living in the bomb shelter and only came out now and then. Mum insisted that we always went home when the All Clear sounded, and I knew why. She wanted to be at home if any news came about Dad.

Tonight, the air raid carried on for a long time. We sat ourselves down in a space on the platform next to Mrs Warburton, a neighbour of ours who spent most of her time in the shelter, and who kept an eye on a couple of mattresses for us to make sure we had somewhere comfortable to stay when we went below ground. Every now and then the walls of the tunnels around us shook slightly when the bombs hit above ground, and the *Boom! Boom!* of explosions sent vibrations along the platforms. Some people started a sing-song a few times to try to raise people's spirits, but most people were tired and just wanted to sleep. After all, this bombing had been going on every night for fourteen nights.

While Annie and I lay down on the mattress, Mum went off to talk to her sister, Theresa, who had her space a bit further along the platform, and had made her patch of platform almost like a room with a couple of garden chairs and a table. Mum knew we'd be safe while we were on the platform, surrounded by people like Mrs Warburton and other friends and neighbours; and she was near enough to see us if we needed her.

"I saw Daddy today," whispered Annie, suddenly.

I looked at her, puzzled.

"Where?" I asked, even though I knew it was impossible that she'd seen Dad.

"In my room," she said. "Just before the air-raid warning."

I looked along the platform and was pleased to see that Mum was still chatting to Aunt Theresa, because I knew she'd get upset if she heard Annie talking like this.

"That wasn't Dad," I said. "It was just your imagination."

"It *was* him," she insisted. "He spoke to me."

"What did he say?" I asked, despite myself.

"I don't know," said Annie. "I couldn't hear. I saw his lips move, but I couldn't hear the words."

Again, I shot a quick look along the platform to make sure that Mum wasn't looking at us. Then I lowered my voice and said firmly:

"Listen, Annie, you mustn't say anything about this."

"To who?"

"To anyone. Not to Mum, or anyone else."

"Is everything all right?"

I looked around, and Mrs Warburton was looking at us, a concerned expression on her face.

"Yes, thank you, Mrs Warburton," I said. "Annie was just feeling a little frightened, because of the bombing."

"Don't you let it worry you, dear," said Mrs Warburton kindly. "Those bombs won't reach us this far below ground. You're quite safe."

"I saw my daddy," said Annie. "In my room."

I let out a silent groan; especially when I saw Mrs Warburton's face go pale. I knew what she was thinking. Some people said that when someone was killed they came and visited the people they loved most as a ghost. There'd been lots of stories like that during the war.

"I told her it's just her imagination," I said hurriedly. "She didn't really."

"I did," said Annie, and her voice raised as she said it again: "I did!"

I saw Mum turn towards us at Annie's raised voice, and I gave her a smile and waved at her.

"It's all right!" I called to her. Then I turned to Mrs Warburton. "I don't think we ought to say anything to Mum, or anyone else. Do you?"

Mrs Warburton swallowed. She still looked pale. She nodded.

"No," she said. "We don't want to say anything that might worry your mum needlessly." She turned to Annie and said, in a kindly voice: "I don't think you should tell anyone else what you saw, Annie."

"Why not?" asked Annie.

"Because…" said Mrs Warburton. Then she dried up. She looked at me, helplessly.

"Because, if Dad came to see you, it must be something that was important just for you," I said, making it up. "If he'd wanted it to be for me and Mum, he'd have come to us as well. I reckon this is a secret he wants to be just between you and him."

"Yes!" said Mrs Warburton. She smiled to Annie. "I reckon Harry's right. It's a secret between you and him. You wouldn't want to ruin that secret by telling, would you?"

"But I've told you," said Annie. "And Harry."

"We won't say anything," I said.

"Not a word," nodded Mrs Warburton. She smiled at Annie again. "I think you ought to go to sleep now, little one. Get so me rest."

There wasn't any need to encourage her more than that. I could see that she was really tired, and now she'd got over the panic of being caught up in the bombing, her tiredness just overcame her. She nodded, and closed her eyes, and within minutes she was fast asleep, just before Mum arrived by us.

"What was all that about?" asked Mum.

I shrugged and forced a smile.

"Nothing," I said. "Just Annie getting a bit loud."

"I hope you weren't upsetting her?" said Mum.

"Nothing like that," said Mrs Warburton with a smile. "Harry was good as gold. I think she was just a little bit tired, that's all." She looked up as the tunnel and the platform shook as another bomb landed close by. "This bombing makes us all a bit edgy, especially the little ones."

Mum nodded, gave the sleeping Annie a kiss, then me one as well, and settled herself down on her mattress to sleep. I closed my eyes and tried to sleep, but I couldn't. All I could think of was what Annie had said about seeing Dad in her room. Was it just her imagination, or was she making it up? She sometimes made up stories, but then that's what little kids do. But if she'd made it up, why didn't she also make up what Dad had said? Had she *really* seen him?

I thought about other stories I'd heard people talking about, about seeing people and finding out later they'd just died. Had she really seen him? If so, did that mean he was ... dead?

I couldn't even think of the word without tears coming into my eyes. No, he couldn't be dead! It was all a story that Annie had made up. Either that, or she'd seen a reflection from a mirror, a shadow, or something like that, which her imagination had turned into Dad.

Please don't let her say anything to Mum, I prayed silently. And please let Dad be alive!

The next morning the All Clear sounded, and me and Mum and Annie made our way up the stairs to street level, along with most of the other people. Some were still staying down below, afraid of what they might find when they came up. I kept hold of Annie's hand as we walked up the stairs, holding onto the banister as we did, ready to shut her up if she started to tell Mum about "seeing Dad". Luckily, Mum was talking to Aunt Theresa most of the way up.

When we came out of the Underground station, we saw how close the bombs had come to the station. The buildings opposite had been destroyed. Now there was just a big hole in the ground, with smoke rising from it, and charred timbers sticking up from where the roof had crashed down and caught fire. The whole place smelt burnt, an acrid smell that got into your nose. I tied a handkerchief around Annie's face to stop the smell and the soot getting into her nose and mouth and choking her, and then did the same for myself. The good thing about this was that, with a hankie tied round her mouth, there was less likelihood of Annie saying anything to Mum about seeing Dad. Till we got home, at least.

We had to walk carefully back along Crowndale Road, because the street was covered in rubble from bombed buildings: smashed bricks, roof tiles, timbers, all with smoke still coming from them. The saddest thing was seeing people's personal belongings lying there: family photographs in frames, the glass smashed; furniture burnt and broken; small things like a doll, or the remains of a book with the cover burnt off. Things that people had treasured, now destroyed.

We turned into Bayham Street and began to walk up towards our house; and then I stopped, a feeling of fear and panic coming over me. Two men in army uniforms stood outside our house, their backs to us.

They've come with the bad news! I thought. They've come to tell Mum that Dad's dead. Annie was right! She did see Dad!

Mum realized that I was hanging back, and she turned and snapped her fingers at me.

"Come on, Harry," she said, impatiently. "We need to get home."

Why can't she see them? I thought, eaten up by pain. She must know what it means! They've come to tell her…

"Meg!"

The voice hit me like a shock. My mouth fell open. The two men had turned round, and one of them was Dad! He came rushing towards us, his arms outstretched.

"Ted!" yelled Mum, and she ran towards him, and they fell into each other's arms.

"Dad!" I called.

Then I was running towards him, dragging Annie along behind me, with her running on her little legs to keep up.

"Harry! Annie!"

Dad grabbed us both up, lifted us off the ground and swung us round. Then he put us down. He gestured towards the other soldier, waving him in. "This is my mate, Arnold."

"They said you was missing at Dunkirk," said my mum, and I could see she was near to tears.

"We were," nodded Dad, grinning. "Me and Arnold couldn't get on the boats, so we came back the long way, behind enemy lines, so to speak."

"Tell me later!" said Mum, and she grabbed Dad again and hugged him.

Annie looked up at me and smiled.

"I told you I saw him," she said. "That's what he was trying to tell me. He was coming home."

1945–1965

The Second World War ended in Europe in May 1945. London, like many other cities, had suffered badly: large areas were flattened by bombing. The area where I was born and grew up, around the Euston/King's Cross/ St Pancras part of central London, was one of them. As a small child I watched diggers and bulldozers level the rubble-strewn areas where houses once stood. The houses were replaced by tower blocks which appeared all over the city to house London's ever-increasing population. And the population itself changed. Before, immigrants had mainly come from Ireland, escaping famine and a lack of work, or places like Russia, escaping persecution. Now they came from all parts of the British Empire – the West Indies, India, Pakistan (although Pakistan didn't exist as a separate country until 1947) and Hong Kong.

Britain had ruled many of these countries for over 100 years, so their citizens were British, and were promised a home in their Mother Nation. Now, as hard times in these countries were made worse by economic difficulties and the threat of war and persecution, many of these Empire citizens took up that promise. New Britons were now all races, all creeds, and that was especially true in London.

As well as this influx of new cultures to the capital, one aspect of British culture spread around the world: football.

Football began as a knock-about game in Britain. By the end of the 19th century it was played mainly by working men as a way of relaxing from the rigours of their jobs. They formed teams at the places where they worked: at Woolwich Arsenal (later Arsenal), at the Crystal Palace.

In England, the home of football was Wembley Stadium in north London. Work on Wembley Stadium began in 1922, and it was completed just in time for the first match there, the FA Cup Final of 1923 between Bolton Wanderers and West Ham United. Bolton won 2-0.

In 1966, Wembley played host to the final of an even more important competition: the World Cup.

World Cup final 1966

Terry Baker and his dad sat side by side on the sofa, their eyes glued to the TV. 30th July 1966, the World Cup Final between England and West Germany at Wembley. On the low coffee table in front of them were packets of crisps and cans of soft drinks, necessary provisions for the game that lay ahead.

In the kitchen, Terry's mum could be heard preparing a cake, which she was intending for them to have for their tea as a post-match celebration. "Providing England win," she said.

"Of course we'll win!" said Mr Baker. "It's at Wembley! A home crowd! And look at our team! Gordon Banks, the best goalkeeper in the world. Bobby Charlton up front! Bobby Moore in the middle!"

Terry wasn't as confident as his dad, although he didn't say as much. Terry still thought that Alf Ramsey, the England Manager, should have put Jimmy Greaves at centre forward. Jimmy Greaves was the best scorer in the League, in Terry's opinion. People said that Ramsey hadn't picked Greaves because he was injured, but Terry wasn't convinced. And even if he did have a bit of a knock, in Terry's opinion, Jimmy Greaves was still the best player England had, injured or not.

Terry shot a look at the clock. Ten to three. The community singing was over. The army bands had gone. The pitch had been cleared. And now there was an enormous roar as the two teams came out, side by side. England, with the captain Bobby Moore at the front, goalie Gordon Banks behind him, then the rest of the team: Bobby Charlton, Geoff Hurst, Roger Hunt, Martin Peters, Alan Ball, Nobby Styles, Jack Charlton, George Cohen, Ray Wilson.

Terry didn't know all the names of the West German, team, just Uwe Seeler, the German captain, and Franz Beckenbauer, who'd both been brilliant in West Germany's previous matches.

The two teams lined up, ready for the presentation to the VIP guest.

"This is gonna be some game," breathed Mr Baker excitedly. "The Germans are good, but we've got that something extra."

The camera showed Bobby Moore, introducing the VIP to the rest of the team, shaking hands … and suddenly the screen went blank.

"Eh?" said Mr Baker, bewildered.

He hurried across to the TV and started knocking it with his knuckles, and tugging at the aerial lead. That had worked before, sometimes, when the picture had vanished.

"Maybe it's the plug?" suggested Terry. "It could be a fuse."

His mum appeared in the doorway.

"The kettle's packed up," she said. "And the fridge is off. I opened the door to get the milk and the light was off, and it's not humming."

"Oh no!" groaned Dad. "What a time for it to happen! Just before kick-off!"

He stood staring at the blank TV screen, a man in shock. His dream of watching the World Cup Final had just been snatched cruelly away from him.

"Maybe Mr Sims will let us watch it on his telly," suggested Terry.

Mr Sims was their next door neighbour.

"Brilliant!" exclaimed Dad. "We might still be in time to see the kick-off!"

He rushed for the front door, shouting at Terry, "Come on, Terry! Bring the crisps!"

They were just about to open the front door, when their doorbell rang. Terry's dad opened the door, and there was Mr Sims. He looked anxious. Behind him stood his two sons, Peter and Bill.

"Mr Baker, can we come in and watch the final on your telly?" he asked urgently. "Our telly's just packed up!"

"So's ours," said Mr Baker. "I was just coming to ask you the same thing!"

"Hey, Mr Baker!" shouted a voice. They turned to look, and saw their neighbour from the other side, Mr Adams, looking out of his window. "Is your telly working?"

"No," said Terry's dad. Then the awful realization hit him. "It's a power cut! The whole street's got no electricity!"

Even as he spoke, men were coming out of their houses on the other side of the road and calling out desperately: "Anyone got a telly that works?"

"It's the whole area!" groaned Mr Baker.

"What are we gonna do, Dad?" asked Bill Sims unhappily.

"We'll go to your Uncle Eric's in Clapham," said Mr Sims. Apologetically, he turned to Mr Baker and said: "Sorry we can't take you with us, only his house is very small."

"We won't take up much room," appealed Mr Baker.

But Mr Sims and his sons had already run off, back to their own house to get their coats.

"Selfish git!" muttered Mr Baker darkly.

"What about Uncle Arthur?" suggested Terry. "If his telly's working we could go there. He's only at Euston. We might miss the first half-hour, but we'd still see the rest."

"Good thinking!" nodded his dad. "I'll go and phone him and make sure they've got power." Then another thought struck him. "In the meantime, go upstairs and tell Penny we need her transistor radio. That's got batteries, so at least we'll be able to listen to the match while we're on our way."

Terry hesitated. His sister, Penny, was sixteen and he was a little bit terrified of her. She considered herself grown-up, and as such she didn't want to have anything to do with her "little kid of a brother", and she told him so. She ran around with a bunch of friends from where she worked, who dressed up like the people they saw in magazines: the girls with back-combed beehive hairdos, black eyeliner, and short miniskirts. Even some of the boys had their long hair back-combed, and they all seemed to wear smart tight trousers and Italian jackets. And they all looked down on him because he was only 12 and just a kid.

"Go on!" Mr Baker urged him. "Go and get her radio off her while I phone Arthur."

Terry headed up the stairs and approached Penny's door with caution. From inside he could hear the sound of pop music, and then a jingle singing out "Radio Caroline!" Radio Caroline was one of the pirate radio stations that broadcast from ships around the coast of England, playing non-stop pop music 24 hours a day.

Terry knocked at Penny's door, then opened it.

Penny was sitting at her dressing table, trying out different types of make-up. Her transistor radio was next to her, playing full blast. Penny looked at him in her dressing table mirror and scowled.

"What do you want?" she demanded.

"There's a power cut," said Terry. "Dad wants to borrow your radio."

"What?" said Penny, shocked, looking at her radio. It was bright pink with an aerial poking upwards from it. "Why?"

"So we can listen to the World Cup Final," said Terry.

Penny turned and looked at him, still shocked.

"Are you mad?" she demanded. "They're going to be playing the new Beatles record today! I can't miss that!"

"Yes, but…" began Terry.

Penny snatched up her precious radio and clutched it possessively.

"No!" she said firmly.

Mr Baker's voice was heard calling from downstairs.

"Arthur's got power!" he called. "Hurry up, Terry! We should get

217

there in time to see the second half! And bring that radio!"

Terry looked at his sister apprehensively.

"It's not my fault," he appealed. "I didn't cause the power cut!"

Penny looked at him, her lower lip trembling. She's going to cry, he thought unhappily. He'd never really seen his sister cry before. Well, not since she'd started work and become an adult.

"You could always go to a friend's and listen to their radio," he suggested.

"Terry!" bellowed his father from downstairs. "Hurry up!"

Penny sat, looking at Terry, misery in her eyes, and then she thrust her precious radio towards Terry.

"If you break it, I'll kill you!" she hissed.

"I won't," Terry assured her.

Clutching the radio, which was now playing the new record by the Beach Boys, "God Only Knows", Terry hurried downstairs. He gave the transistor radio to his dad, who looked at it, affronted.

"Why haven't you got it on the football?" he demanded.

"I didn't have time," said Terry, grabbing his coat and putting it on.

Mr Baker started twiddling with the knob, trying to find the BBC Light Programme and the football commentary. As he did, he called out to the kitchen to his wife: "Me and Terry are off to Arthur's, Marge! He's got power and a telly that works!"

Mrs Baker appeared from the kitchen.

"But he's right over at Euston," she said, puzzled.

"Yes, but this is the World Cup Final!" said Mr Baker. "England against West Germany. I can't miss this!"

"It'll be on the telly in the window in the shop in the High Street," suggested Mrs Baker. "You could watch it there."

"Stand in the street?" said Mr Baker. "And there'll be no sound!"

"Yes, but you can see what's happening," pointed out Mrs Baker.

"It's not the same," said Mr Baker. "Come on, Terry. Let's get to the bus stop!"

And he hurried out, the radio pressed to his ear as he ran, Terry close behind him. Terry heard his mum sigh and say, "Stupid men!" Then the front door closed.

Terry and his dad ran, and suddenly Mr Baker skidded to a halt.

"They've scored!" he said, shocked.

"Who?" asked Terry, but he could tell from the stunned expression on his dad's face.

"The Germans!" said Mr Baker. "Haller just scored. Twelve minutes!" He turned up the volume and then broke into a run. As Terry ran after him, he could hear the commentator saying: "So there we have it. Siegfried Held sent a cross into the penalty area and Ray Wilson headed it out, but it went straight to Helmut Haller, who smashed it into the net, past Jack Charlton and goalkeeper Gordon Banks. England nil, West Germany one."

They reached the bus stop. For once, there wasn't much of a queue. Terry guessed it was because most people were already in place, watching or listening to the Final. No one was doing much travelling today.

Terry and his family lived in Holloway, and Uncle Arthur lived in

Somers Town, which was next to Euston station, a twenty-minute ride on the 91 bus from Holloway, depending on the traffic. Terry wondered how long they'd have to wait for the bus. Sometimes one turned up straight away, sometimes they had to wait a quarter of an hour. It all added to the delay before they could sit and watch the match. Terry looked at his dad's watch. Nearly twenty past three. Half time would be at 3.45. If a bus came along soon they should still be able to get to Uncle Arthur's in time for the second half. Terry strained to listen to the commentary coming from the radio, and then he heard the commentator shout: "And Hurst has scored!"

"Yes!" yelled Mr Baker and Terry together in joy.

The commentator continued: "Overath gave away a free kick which Bobby Moore delivered with great accuracy into the West German goal area, and Geoff Hurst headed the ball past Tilkowski into the German goal. One-one."

"Brilliant!" beamed Mr Baker happily. "Now we're motoring!"

"The bus is coming, Dad!" called Terry.

He put out his hand, the bus pulled up, and Terry and his dad hurried up to the top deck. Terry preferred riding on the top deck of a bus – if he sat at the very front he could imagine that he was piloting an aeroplane, flying over London. Luckily, the front seats were empty, and they settled down, the radio between them, listening to the commentary from Wembley.

The bus moved off, and then there was the sound of heavy footsteps from behind them.

"Fares!" barked the conductor.

Mr Baker handed over some change.

"One and a half to Euston," he said.

The conductor rolled off the tickets and handed them over, then announced: "And you can turn that thing off."

Terry and his dad looked at the conductor, blankly.

"What?" asked Mr Baker.

The conductor pointed to a sign that said: "No radios allowed. Respect your fellow travellers."

Dad gaped at the sign, and at the conductor, and then pointed at Penny's bright pink transistor radio.

"But it's the World Cup Final!" he protested.

"I don't care about that!" snapped the conductor. "I hate football!"

"It's England and West Germany!" said Mr Baker.

"It's a radio," said the conductor sourly, "and rules are rules. No radios. Now either turn it off, or you can get off."

"But we've just paid our fares!" protested Mr Baker.

"And now I'm telling you to turn that radio off," said the conductor.

"You might have told us the rules before you took our money!" said Mr Baker, upset.

Once again, the conductor pointed to the sign.

"It's there," he said. "In black and white."

"Actually it's in red and yellow," said Terry. Because the small poster had red lettering on a yellow background.

The bus conductor glared at Terry.

"If you're gonna be funny I'll turn you off this bus anyway," he said.

"I wasn't being funny..." protested Terry.

His dad stopped him.

"All right, I'll turn it off," he said, and he clicked the volume knob off. The conductor gave them another scowl, and then walked off, heading for the stairs at the back.

Mr Baker looked enquiringly at Terry.

"Didn't Penny have any of those earpiece things, so you can hear it without anyone else listening to it?" he asked.

Terry shook his head.

"Not that I saw," he said. "She likes to keep it as loud as possible."

"You're telling me," said his dad with a sigh. He looked towards the back of the bus, checking that the conductor was out of sight. Then he raised the transistor radio to his ear and switched it on, but with the volume on so low Terry could hardly hear it. Terry leaned it, and could just make out the commentator's voice as he said: "Emmerich brings the ball down the left wing, but Nobby Stiles comes in with a tackle..."

"I can see you!" bellowed the voice of the conductor from downstairs.

Terry and his dad looked up guiltily, and saw the conductor's glaring expression reflected in the mirror in the front corner of the bus, just above their heads.

Mr Baker gave a sigh and reluctantly switched the transistor off.

It was four o'clock as they reached the front door of Uncle Arthur's flat in the small block in Somers Town.

"The second half's just about to start," said Uncle Arthur, ushering them in.

"What's the score?" asked Mr Baker.

"One-all," said Uncle Arthur.

Good, thought Terry, we haven't missed any more goals.

Uncle Arthur's small living room was packed with men, all friends of Arthur's.

"Shove up on that settee!" called Arthur. "My brother's here with my nephew. Make room!"

There was some grumbling from the men packed onto the settee, but they squeezed up enough so that Terry could squash himself into a space.

"I'll grab the floor," said Mr Baker, and he dropped down onto the floor next to the settee, just as the referee's whistle blew for the start of the second half.

Terry was gripped by the game, which went from one end of the pitch to the other, with each side threatening to score, and the defence smothering the shots. With just twelve minutes left, England launched yet another attack. Alan Ball passed to Geoff Hurst, who fired a shot at the West German goal, but a German defender blocked it and pushed the ball out, straight to the feet of Martin Peters, who slammed the ball past the West German keeper into the net.

Goal!

The crowd of men in Arthur's small flat went mad, shouting and cheering.

"That's it!" roared Mr Baker. "2-1. Twelve minutes to go! It's all over! It's ours!"

But the shouting and cheering stopped as soon as the game restarted, and the West Germans attacked with a new ferocity, and now England were defending as the West Germans sought to batter the ball into the English goal.

"Hang on, lads!" muttered the man next to Terry nervously. Terry looked at the clock. 89 minutes. One minute to go. *Hang on*, he added silently. *Just a few seconds to go...*

The sound of the referee's whistle sent shock waves through the men in the room. The England players were in their goal areas, protesting to the referee.

"What happened?" asked one man.

"The ref's given a free kick against Jack Charlton," said Uncle Arthur. "For pulling down Seeler."

"But Seeler backed into Jackie!" said Mr Baker, outrage in his voice. "That referee's blind! The foul was the other way."

"Ssssh!" said one of the men.

All the men fell silent and the tense atmosphere in the tiny living room was stretched to breaking point as Lothar Emmerich readied himself to take the West German free kick. The left winger struck it, and George Cohen, the English right back, blocked it, but the ball bounced out. In a flash, Weber, the West German centre back was onto the ball, and his kick sent the ball past Banks and into the English goal.

Terry saw Gordon Banks turn to the referee and protest, pointing to one of the West German players, as the Germans began celebrating.

"It hit his hand!" cried the man next to Terry indignantly. "The ball hit Schnellinger's hand! It's not a goal! It's handball! A free kick to England!"

But the referee had blown his whistle and was pointing to the centre spot; and then almost immediately blew it again to signal the end of the game.

2-2. A draw.

"Extra time," said Terry's dad hollowly. "It ain't fair!"

The extra time of that game was the most exciting of any football game that Terry had ever seen. For ten minutes both sides attacked again and again, but each time the ball was cleared by the defenders and sent back up the pitch into the opposing team's half. And then, in the eleventh minute, Alan Ball gave chase to a long ball that had been sent up the field by the English defence. He caught it just by the right-hand West German corner flag, and lobbed it from there into the six-yard box, where Geoff Hurst was waiting. Hurst caught it on the turn and knocked the ball past the German goalkeeper. It went up, hit the underside of the crossbar, came down, and then bounced out, and the West German full back headed the ball behind the goal.

"Goal!" roared Terry's dad. "It crossed the line!"

"Yes!" yelled the other men in loud delight.

On the screen, the England forwards, Hunt and Charlton, were already celebrating, arms raised aloft in triumph. But the West Germans were protesting. Terry could tell from their gestures to the referee they were claiming that the ball hadn't crossed the line, that it had bounced out and been headed away. The referee hesitated, then he walked over to the linesman, the one who raised his flag to indicate a goal had been scored.

A tense silence fell in the room, as it did all over Wembley.

"It crossed the line!" whispered Uncle Arthur hoarsely.

But Terry wasn't so sure. The ball *might* have crossed the goal line, but it might also have come down on the goal line and bounced out. He couldn't be sure.

They watched in agonized silence as the referee and the linesman had a brief whispered conversation. Then they saw the linesman point his flag at the centre circle, and the referee put his whistle to his lips and blew, also pointing in the same direction.

It was a goal! England 3, West Germany 2!

The men in the room went wild, leaping up and down and shouting in delight, and Terry was worried he was going to be crushed when they stopped jumping around and sat down on the sofa again; but the whistle for the restart and the kick-off by West Germany brought silence to the room again.

From then on, the West Germans launched attack after attack, while the England players battled them in defence.

As the clock ticked down into the very last minute of extra time, the West German defenders joined their forwards in the English half of the field to intensify the attack. A stray ball came to Bobby Moore, who booted a long pass to Geoff Hurst on the left wing. With most of the West German team in the English half, Hurst was unmarked, and he began to rush up the field towards the West German goal as the final seconds ticked down. Terry could see that some English supporters had already clambered over the barriers and were heading towards the pitch, leaping about as if the game was already over. Terry heard the commentator say: "And here comes Hurst. There are some people on the pitch. They think it's all over." And then, as Terry watched, Geoff Hurst hit a spectacular shot that flew past the West German goalie into the back of the net, and the commentator added: "It is now! It's four!"

Four goals to two!

Terry couldn't hear the sound of the referee's whistle above the yelling and cheering. He wondered how the people in the flats below and above Uncle Arthur were feeling at this yelling and hooting and stamping of feet. If they had any sense they'd have gone out for the day.

"Yes!" exulted his dad, punching the air. "YES!" He turned and grinned at Terry. "I always knew we'd win!" he beamed. Then he let out a big long happy sigh. "I think we can go home now and tuck into that celebration cake your mum's made."

1967–2011

During the 1960s, London was known as Swinging London. Oxford Street, from Tottenham Court Road to Marble Arch, became the Shopping Capital of Europe, and Soho acted like a magnet to the movers and shakers of the arts world.

The world of money and international finance, however, was moving from the ancient City of London to the modern skyscrapers of the new developments at Canary Wharf and the Isle of Dogs.

As some parts of London's skyline changed, others remained firmly the same: St Paul's Cathedral, Westminster Abbey, the Houses of Parliament, Buckingham Palace.

The real change was in the make-up of the population. Decades of immigration, and international companies setting up key offices in London, resulted in a cosmopolitan mix. Although the majority (57.7%) of London's 7.6 million population still described themselves as "White British" in the 2001 Census, the rest of London's residents came from a wide variety of backgrounds. According to the Office of National Statistics, London's population was made up of 248,000 people from India; 122,000 from Poland; 110,000 from the Republic of Ireland; 107,000 from Bangladesh; 95,000 from Nigeria; as well as people from Jamaica (80,000), Nigeria (69,000), Pakistan (67,000), Kenya (66,000), Sri Lanka (50,000), Ghana (46,000), Cyprus (46,000), South Africa (45,000), the USA (44,000), Australia (41,000), Germany (40,000), Turkey (39,000), Italy (38,000), France (38,000), Somalia (34,000), Uganda (32,000), New Zealand (27,000), and many other countries. Since the 2001 Census, London has seen an even bigger influx of people from Eastern Europe.

It is for this reason that Lord Coe was able to say proudly, when London was chosen as the venue for the 2012 Olympics, that every competing country would already have its citizens and supporters living there, ready and keen to urge their ancestor country on to victory, and to gold.

Olympic dreams 2012

On your marks!

Andrene Baker settled herself into her starting blocks – but the last thing she felt was "settled". She felt frightened, excited, nervous, exhilarated, so many emotions all at once. At sixteen years old she was in the final of the women's 200 metres at the Olympic Games, in London, her home city.

OK, she'd got into the final as Fastest Loser, which meant she was in Lane 8, which everyone said was the worst lane draw for the race. But she was here, in the final. Her mum and dad were in the crowd, watching. She knew they'd be on the edge of their seats the whole time. In fact, dad would be standing once the race began, shouting and screaming, with the people behind him telling him to sit down, and Mum would be clinging onto his arm, her eyes fixed on the track. Andrene knew because they'd done exactly that when they'd watched her in the qualifying rounds and the semi-finals. She'd seen them on the TV replays.

They'd also be arguing about which of them Andrene had inherited her running talent from. Mum said it was from her. She said that when she was at school she always won races at sports day, and if she hadn't

231

broken her leg in her teens, she could have competed at the top level. Dad countered this by saying that when *he'd* been at school he'd also won races sports day. Although, under pressure, he admitted that had been at Junior School, and then he'd only won the egg and spoon race. But he added that he'd been the top scorer in his school football team, too.

To Andrene, it didn't matter. What mattered was that *she* was here, on this track at the Olympic Stadium, as one of the fastest women in the world. Alongside her, the other runners were taking their places, stretching as they put themselves into their blocks. Two Jamaicans, one from Trinidad, two Americans, one from Germany, one from France. And Andrene for Great Britain.

Next to Andrene in Lane 7 was the Frenchwoman; then one of the Americans, then the Trinidadian, then a Jamaican, another American, another Jamaican, and – on the far side in Lane 1 – the German.

Don't think about them, Andrene told herself. But it was hard not to. One of the Jamaicans was the World Champion, and one of the Americans the fastest qualifier. Every other woman in this line had run faster than her. And Andrene's time as Fastest Loser had been her personal best.

It doesn't matter, she urged herself. *What matters is now. The next thirty seconds.*

She took a deep breath and closed her eyes for a second, visualizing herself running.

This is my home. This track, this stadium, was built in my home town. I am more than just a Londoner, I am an East Londoner. Hackney, her birthplace and her home, was just a few miles from the very spot where she was now standing. Everyone she knew in Hackney would be watching her right now. Not just Hackney, the whole of London, the whole of Great Britain would be watching her, willing her on. She felt the weight of expectation. Her coach had warned her about it.

"Ignore it", he'd said. "You don't need to get bogged down with what the other runners can and can't do; what they've achieved, records they've won. That was then, this is NOW."

Set!

Andrene pushed herself up, body poised, balanced on her toes and the tips of her fingers.

Please don't let there be a false start, she prayed silently. In the shorter races, a hundredth of a second could be the difference between winning and losing, so everyone threw themselves forward at the sound of the starter's gun. Poised, trembling on the brink, ready to go, and it only needed one wobble, one slight overbalance, one flicker of movement out of the corner of the eye, the imagined sound of the gun going off, to trigger movement just a split second too soon. She'd done it herself at other meetings. But she was determined that wasn't going to happen here, not in the final. There was too much at stake.

She had to get out of her blocks at exactly right moment; too slow and the race was lost; a millisecond too soon, and her race would be over before it had begun.

The tension of holding her position, leaning forward, but not so far she'd overbalance, made her muscles scream in silent agony.

Fire the gun! She urged. *Fire the gun!* Why was the starter taking so long? Surely one of the girls would overbalance during this delay. *Please, fire the gun!*

Bang!

As the starter's gun went off, Andrene hurled herself out of her blocks, head low, legs driving, arms pumping. The crowd were screaming and cheering, driving their favourites on, but Andrene knew that most of the yells of encouragement were for her, Andrene. This was her home turf. The crowd was her home crowd.

She drove on, running hard, a wall of sound enveloping her as she ran, her head coming up now as she got into her stride. No, more than just her stride ... *faster* than her stride. She was flying, faster than she'd ever run before. She didn't know where the other runners were, for all she knew they were hanging on her tail, ready to hurtle past her at the bend. She couldn't hear them because of the sheer volume of the sound of the crow shouting and screaming; the stadium was a cauldron of intense, deafening noise.

Ignore the others. Run your own race. Run fast, as fast as you've ever run. Breathe. Legs and arms moving together, like a machine. I am a machine, she thought. There was no air in her throat, her thigh and calf muscles screamed with pain, her joints felt as if they were being torn apart... *I am running the fastest I have ever run!*

Into the bend, eyes straight ahead, not looking to her left to see where the others were, no distractions. *Just run, run ... run hard, run hard ... drive on...*

She was aware of a flash of colour just to her left … near her… lane 7 catching her… *Run faster! Run faster!*

Teeth gritted, lungs bursting, heart pumping, joints crunching as her feet pounded, every muscle, every ligament, every nerve, every sinew tearing and stretching … *I am the fastest I am the fastest I am the fastest…*

Out of the bend into the final straight … aware of a presence next to her, running neck and neck, level … the closing seconds … the line ahead…!

A final surge. A thrust, dip down, neck muscles stretched, whole body stretching…

The roar of the crowd!!! Enough to raise the stadium, lift it from the ground and soar it upwards into space.

A gabble of voices around her. Andrene turned to the giant screen showing the instant replay…

Yes! She'd done it! She'd won by the barest margin, a hair's breadth … but she'd won!

She felt stunned. Her legs were like jelly. They screamed pain, she wanted to fall down, but her brain told her, *No: Stand. This is your moment!*

The screaming in the stadium was subsiding. The other women were coming up to her. Hugs. Smiles. Genuine smiles. They knew what this meant to her.

She looked again at the giant screen. There was the result, over the replay of her hurtling forward over the line: *First: Andrene Baker.*

Gold!

2012 and onwards

Just like the ever-changing and ever-growing Baker family, London is a constantly changing, constantly growing city.

From that small Stone Age settlement on the marshes by the great river, through Roman Londinium, the Saxon city, the imposing city castles and cathedrals of Norman conquest, medieval London, the massive influx of people with industrial London in Victorian times, and then modern London, this is a city that never stands still.

Where now for this great city? That is for Londoners themselves to decide.

Places in the stories

Buckingham Palace

Buckingham Palace is the residence of the British Royal family. It started out as Buckingham House, built by the Duke of Buckingham in 1705. King George III bought the house in 1761 as a private residence for his wife, Queen Charlotte, and when George IV became king in 1820, he decided to turn Buckingham House into a palace. He commissioned the architect, John Nash, to carry out the work. The expense of the rebuilding work escalated, and by 1829 it had cost half a million pounds. In 1830 George V died, and his younger brother, William IV, became King. Concerned about the ever-increasing costs, William sacked Nash as architect of the project and replaced him with Edward Blore, whose ideas for the rest of the building were less expensive.

However, William never lived in Buckingham Palace. Queen Victoria was the first monarch to live there when she became queen in 1837.

By the end of the 19th century the front of the palace was showing serious signs of deterioration because the chemicals in London's sooty atmosphere had eaten away at the soft French stone. In 1913 it was decided to replace the ruined façade at the front with much harder Portland stone, a process that took over a year to complete.

The forecourt of the palace, where the Changing of the Guard takes place, was created in 1911. In the same year the gates and railings were put in place at the front of the palace.

Charing Cross station/ Hungerford Stairs

Hungerford Stairs was just one of a series of stairs used by watermen who ferried passengers across (and along) the river Thames. These stairs were used at high tide as safe places for boatmen to pick up passengers. As well as the watermen's stairs at Hungerford, such stairs (or pick-up points) could be found at many places on both side of the Thames, such as Parliament, Westminster, Whitehall, Savoy, Temple, Blackfriars Bridge and Limehouse.

Hungerford Stairs were by the site of Hungerford Market. There had been a market on this site, housed in a large building, since 1680. In 1854 the building was damaged by fire, and the markets closed. In 1862 the derelict building was sold to the South-Eastern Railway Company, who built Charing Cross railway station on the site. The railway station opened in 1864.

Cornhill

Cornhill is one of the highest and oldest parts of the City of London. St Michael's Church in Cornhill, designed by Sir Christopher Wren, is built on the site of the Roman forum of old Londinium.

London's first mechanically-pumped public water supply was built at the junction of Cornhill and Leadenhall Street in 1582. This became the mark from which distances from and to London were measured.

Crystal Palace

The Crystal Palace was the name given to the massive glass and iron structure erected in London's Hyde Park to house the Great Exhibition of 1851.

After the Exhibition finished, the palace was taken down and rebuilt at Sydenham in south London in 1854. In 1936 the building was destroyed by fire, but it still gives its name to that area of London. The Crystal Palace football team was formed by workers from the Crystal Palace in 1905.

Globe Theatre

The Globe Theatre on Bankside, by the Thames, is a modern reconstruction of the old Globe Theatre of Shakespeare's day. It was opened in 1997, and stands about 200 metres from the site of the original.

The original Globe Theatre was built by Cuthbert and Richard Burbage in 1598-9. It was only used for performances during the summer months, as – apart from the stage and the galleries – it had no roof to protect the audience from bad weather. Shakespeare's plays *Richard II, Romeo and Juliet, King Lear, Othello, Henry VIII, Love's Labours Lost, The Winter's Tale, The Taming of the Shrew* and *Macbeth,* were all performed at the Globe during Shakespeare's lifetime.

In 1613 the theatre was destroyed by fire when cannons used to create a dramatic effect during *Henry VIII* accidentally set the thatched roof of the stage and galleries alight. It was rebuilt and re-opened in 1614. In 1642 the Puritans closed it in their campaign against "lewd displays", and the Globe was demolished in 1644.

The Houses of Parliament (also known as **The Palace of Westminster**)
The first Palace of Westminster was built for Edward the Confessor.
After Edward's death and the Norman Conquest in 1066, William the
Conqueror adopted it as his palace. The Palace of Westminster remained
the main residence for the Kings of England for the next 400 years, until
Henry VIII removed the royal court to his preferred site at Hampton
Court. But the Palace of Westminster remained the administrative centre
of England.

Until Edward I's death in 1307, the Kings Council met in
Westminster Hall. After that, the Lords and the Commons held their
meetings separately, establishing a tradition that continues today.

In 1834, fire destroyed most of the Palace of Westminster.
Construction of a new building began in 1837. The House of Lords was
opened in 1847, and the House of Commons in 1851. The Clock Tower
(more popularly known as Big Ben) was completed in 1858.

During the Second World War, the building was severely damaged
during air raids; with much of the House of Commons being reduced
to rubble. It was rebuilt between 1945 and 1950.

London Bridge
London Bridge connects the city of London on the north side of the
Thames to Southwark on the south side. Until Putney Bridge opened in
1729, London Bridge was the only bridge across the Thames.

It is believed that a bridge across the Thames has existed at this place since the Romans first arrived almost 2,000 years ago. A simple wooden bridge was constructed by the Romans in about AD 50, and replaced by a stronger wooden bridge in about AD 55. This was destroyed by Boudicca's army, along with most of the rest of London, in AD 61. Throughout the history of London, a succession of bridges have been constructed at this crossing point, all of which were destroyed or fell into disrepair, and were then replaced by newer and stronger versions.

The current London Bridge was opened in 1973.

The London Underground

The London Underground (known as the Tube) is the oldest underground railway in the world. The first section opened in 1863, and now forms the Circle, Hammersmith & City, and Metropolitan lines. In 1890 it became the first to use electric trains.

The London Underground has 402 kilometres of track and serves 270 stations. It is the second longest metro system in the world (after the Shanghai Metro). During weekdays about 3.5 million people a day use the London Underground.

During the Second World War Londoners used their local Tube stations as air-raid shelters. At first the authorities tried to discourage people from sleeping in Tube stations, but when they saw how many lives they saved they began to fit them out so they could be lived in, putting in bunks, latrines and catering facilities.

The deepest station is Hampstead, on the Northern Line, with a lift shaft 55.2 metres deep.

London Wall

The first London Wall was built by the Romans at some time between AD 200 and 220 as a defence against attack. The wall was built with mainly Kentish ragstone brought to London from Maidstone along the Thames. The original wall was 5 kilometres (3 miles) long, about 6 metres (20 feet) high, and 2–3 (6–9 feet) metres wide. It had a number of gates built into it: from west to east there were: Ludgate, Newgate, Cripplegate, Bishopsgate and Aldgate. Aldersgate was added in about AD 350, and Moorgate was built during medieval times.

During the 18th and 19th centuries large parts of the wall were demolished to make way for new buildings. All that remains of the wall nowadays are fragments, the best examples of which are in the grounds of the Museum of London and by Tower Hill.

Marshalsea debtors' prison

Based at Southwark, on the south bank of the Thames, Marshalsea was a prison from 1329 until it closed in 1842. It housed political prisoners, but it was best known for being a debtors' prison. Debtors were allowed to leave during the day so they could work to pay off their debts, but had to return to the prison each night before the gates were locked.

Marshalsea was made famous by Charles Dickens in his novel *Little Dorrit*, which was based on his own experience – his father was imprisoned there for debt. Much of the prison was demolished in the 1870s, though some parts of the buildings were left standing and were used by small firms into the 20th century.

Monument

This structure is 61 metres tall, and was erected on the order of Charles II to mark the spot where the Great Fire of London of 1666 broke out. It was designed by Christopher Wren and Robert Hook. (See also **Pudding Lane**.) Another monument, the Golden Boy of Pye Corner in Smithfield, marks the spot where the Great Fire is said to have stopped.

Olympic Stadium and Park

The Stadium for the London 2012 Olympic and Paralympic Games in Stratford, East London, was built on the site of a former industrial island between the River Lea, the Old Pudding Mill River, and the City River Mill. The Stadium was built to hold 80,000 spectators, and will convert to a 25,000-seater permanent stadium following the London Olympics.

The Olympic Park is the name given to the overall sporting complex, which includes the Olympic Stadium, the Aquatic Centre, the Velodrome, the basketball and handball arenas, and the Olympic Village to house the athletes.

Following the Olympic Games in 2013, the site will be renamed Queen Elizabeth Olympic Park. The Olympic Park and newly-renovated Stratford City have been given the postcode E20, which was previously a fictional postcode used for the area of Walford in the TV soap-opera *Eastenders*.

Pudding Lane

Pudding Lane got its name from the medieval word used to describe the entrails and guts of animals. Pudding Lane was the route by which these guts and entrails were taken from the butchers' shops in Eastcheap to the dung barges on the Thames. The Great Fire of London started at Farriner's Bakery in Pudding Lane at about midnight on 2 September 1666.

St Pancras station

Work on St Pancras station began in 1863, and the long glass and iron train shed was completed in 1867.

The Midland Grand Hotel which fronted the station along Euston Road, was finished in 1872.

Between 2003 and 2007 the station was developed to become one of the largest railway termini in Europe. It is the major point of embarkation for Eurostar and train journeys through the Channel Tunnel.

St Paul's Cathedral

St Paul's Cathedral, with its domed roof, is one of the most recognizable buildings in London. It stands on the top of Ludgate Hill, and from 1710 to 1962 it was the tallest building in London.

It is believed that there has been a cathedral dedicated to St Paul on this site since AD 604. The present cathedral was designed by Sir Christopher Wren, and was built to replace the cathedral destroyed in the Great Fire of London in 1666.

Many famous people have been buried at St Paul's Cathedral, or have memorials there. They include Christopher Wren (who was the first to be buried there in 1723), Lord Kitchener, the Duke of Wellington, Lord Nelson, Sir Winston Churchill, Florence Nightingale, and J M W Turner.

Seven Dials

In mid-Victorian times, the Seven Dials area of London near to Covent Garden was a notorious slum, a "rookery". It was originally developed by Thomas Neale in the early 1690s as a place for the well-to-do to live, with seven roads converging at one junction. A column was erected at the point where the roads met. Each side of the column had a sundial facing a different road. The original sundial column was taken down in 1773, as the area deteriorated and the authorities feared it might get damaged.

Today, Seven Dials is a prosperous shopping area. The sundial column was re-constructed in 1989, to the original design, and unveiled by Queen Beatrix of the Netherlands.

Strand

The Strand is one of London's most famous streets, running from Trafalgar Square in the west to Aldwych in the east. The name "strand" means bank or shore, and at one time this street was on the northern shore of the River Thames, before the river was narrowed by building on land reclaimed from the river.

Between the 16th and 19th centuries, the Strand housed some of London's finest buildings belonging to the aristocracy. Two of them are still standing: Somerset House, and the Savoy Hotel, which was built on the site of the Savoy Palace.

Tower of London

William the Conqueror started building the Tower of London's White Tower in 1078 as a way of enforcing Norman rule over England.

At first it was a royal residence; but as time passed it became better known as a highly secure prison. Many notable people were imprisoned here, including Princess Elizabeth (later Queen Elizabeth I), Walter Raleigh, Anne Boleyn, Lady Jane Grey and Rudolf Hess.

Over time, the Tower has been expanded on the orders of different kings, particularly Richard the Lionheart, Henry III and Edward I.

The Tower of London is also the place where the Crown Jewels are kept. It is believed Henry III started the tradition of keeping them at the Tower. After King Charles I was deposed in 1649, the Crown Jewels were disposed of. When the monarchy was restored in 1660 the only items that had survived were three ceremonial swords and a teaspoon, so the Crown Jewels were remade.

In 1669 the Crown Jewels were moved to the Martin Tower and put on display for the public; and in 1671 Captain Thomas Blood attempted to steal them, but was foiled.

The Crown Jewels are currently stored in the Waterloo Barracks at the Tower.

Wembley Stadium

The original Wembley Stadium, famous for its Twin Towers, opened in 1923, just in time for the FA Cup Final between Bolton Wanderers and West Ham United, which Bolton won 2-0. In 1966, Wembley played host to the Final of an even more important competition: the World Cup.

In 2003 the old Wembley Stadium was demolished, and a new stadium was constructed on the site. The new Wembley Stadium opened in 2007. It has a capacity of 90,000, and is the second largest stadium in Europe. The stadium is owned by the English Football Association.

Westminster Abbey

The site where Westminster Abbey stands was considered a holy place long before a cathedral was built there. Legend has it that a fisherman called Aldrich saw a vision of St Peter near the site at Thorn Island, and following his vision he and other fishermen made plentiful catches of salmon in the river. As a result, the Bishop of London, Mellitus, consecrated the site as holy in 624. The image of the salmon in the Chapter House floor relates to this legend of the salmon fishers.

In the early 970s St Dunstan, through King Edgar, gave the site to an order of Benedictine monks who built a wooden abbey on this spot.

In 1045 Edward the Confessor ordered the construction of an abbey on the site, made of stone. The building took many years, and it was finally consecrated on 28 December 1065. A week later, Edward the Confessor died.

The Abbey became the place of coronation for England's kings, beginning with the Norman conqueror, William I. In 1245 Henry II ordered the rebuilding of the Abbey as the major monumental building of the age, employing three master masons to oversee the building. By the time Henry died in 1272, most of the building work on the Abbey was completed.

Further additions were made to the Abbey throughout the centuries that followed.

In 1658 Oliver Cromwell was given an elaborate funeral at the Abbey, but in 1661 his body was dug up and hanged from a nearby gibbet.

The two western towers of the Abbey were constructed between 1722 and 1745 under the direction of the architect, Nicholas Hawksmoor.